By William Rubin

Forbidden Beginnings:
Jacqueline's Tragedy

Forbidden Birth

Forbidden Cure

Michelle's Captivity

A CHRIS RAVELLO MEDICAL THRILLER

MICHELLE'S CAPTIVITY

OMNIBUS EDITION

WILLIAM RUBIN

Crystal Vision
Publishing

ISBN: 978-1-949189-97-1

Published by Crystal Vision Publishing
Cover design by Carl Graves ♦ Extended Imagery
Design and formatting by Christine Keleny ♦
CKBooks Publishing

The gem cannot be polished without friction,
nor man perfected without trials.
~ Confucius

MICHELLE'S CAPTIVITY 1

MIRROR, MIRROR

PROLOGUE

Michelle's heart pounds with fear as she tears down the stairwell. Rick's boots hammer ever closer, each reverberation amplifying her anxiety as she dodges gaps in the rotted wood. Lunging onto the next landing, she stumbles and slams into the floor. Panic overtakes her as she scrambles to her feet with Rick bearing down on her. *One more set of stairs, then I can outrun him on the street!* But Michelle's heart sinks as the front door flies open. Tony comes crashing in, gun drawn. His beady eyes lock in on Michelle, unaware Rick is close behind her.

Only one chance to get out of this alive. Michelle pauses a split second, waiting till Rick is almost on top of her but still out of Tony's line of sight. *It's now or never. Here goes...*

▹ Chapter 1 ◃

Saturday, October 10th, 2015

Adorned in her favorite black sportswear, Michelle Ravello laces up her bright pink Hoka running shoes and smiles. Since freshman year in high school, when she discovered how good she was in track and field, she's been a dedicated runner. A good, long run is just what she needs right now to melt away the stress.

She straps Christine, age four, and James, age three, into the back seat of her Honda Odyssey and smiles brightly. "Be good today and we can go for ice cream later," she says with enthusiasm.

"Sundaes! Hudson Creamery, Mommy—please!" Christine pleads. James nods. "Yeah, chocolate." Michelle offers a wary smile. "Okay, but only if you're good while Mommy's working out."

"We'll be good!" rings the chorus as Michelle

finishes adjusting the car seat straps and hops in the front seat.

Heading south on Route 9, Michelle admires the beauty of the Hudson River off to her right and the rolling hills of Rockland County just beyond. The river, its tranquil, still waters dotted by the last of the season's sailboats, is one of the few bright spots in their lives this past year and a welcome distraction from her troubling thoughts. Michelle shakes her head. Growing up in Yonkers, across from the sprawling grounds of Untermeyer Park with its Persian Paradise Garden and Grecian architecture, the Hudson was never far from her, yet always seemed just out of reach.

"Mommy, are we there yet?" Christine chirps.

"No, pumpkin, we just left Peekskill." She smiles at Christine through the rearview mirror. "Do you remember where Mommy's going to work out today?"

Christine giggles. "Rockafella Preserve?" she says with caution.

Michelle makes a show of looking at the passenger seat next to her, occupied only by her handbag and a gym bag containing a change of clothes, shoes, and her toiletries. "No Daddy today, sweetie. So we'll go to a gym where people can watch you while Mommy is busy."

James looks at Christine, then Michelle, perplexed at the exchange.

"Club Fit!" Christine yells as James's eyes go big

at the thought of a visit to the club's fabled childcare facility, The Energy Center.

"Very good, sweetie. Just a little bit longer."

The blue minivan glides past the exit for Buchanan, a small village in Westchester County, New York nestled on the banks of the Hudson and best known for its soon-to-be-shuttered nuclear power plant at Indian Point.

Michelle's face takes on a darker hue as her mind churns over the tragedy that changed all of their lives forever—Jacqueline Ravello's terrible mugging at the gates of The Bronx Botanical Gardens last August. That attack on her mother-in-law, and what followed, lead to a cataclysmic sea change in her family's life.

Gone is the big house overlooking the Long Island Sound in Rye and Chris's promising career as a NYC surgeon. In their place, a modest old home in Peekskill they can afford on her husband's meager salary as the lead detective and chief of the NYPD's newly minted Division of Medical Crimes.

Michelle takes a deep breath and scans the road ahead and behind, her wavy, raven ponytail bouncing about as apprehension gnaws at her. Her left hand jumps nervously to her neck, her fingertips tracing the jagged scar there. She squints at the rearview mirror as her eyelid twitches. Has that black car been following her the whole time or is she just being paranoid? She pulls into the left lane and accelerates past three cars before settling in front of an old, green Passat Wagon. Exhaling, her hands tremble on the wheel. With the serial killer, Dr. Jean Louis Durand, still on the loose, no one is safe, least of all her. He made that crystal clear at their ill-fated meeting back in early July when Durand nearly killed her. Her hand reflexively traces the scar again as she curses under her breath.

The Passat falls back as Michelle puts Dr. Harlow's instructions into motion, calming herself with slow, deep rhythmic breaths and reassuring thoughts. *Who'd want to tail a mom and her kids in a minivan?* She chuckles as she chastises herself. *Just being silly, right?*

The black car appears again, steadily passing others before it settles in front of the Passat.

Michelle's pulse quickens as her knuckles turn white on the wheel. That settles it. The hell with relaxation techniques! She grabs her iPhone and runs through the list in her head. Her girlfriends would drop everything to help her, but when push comes to shove, how much could they really help right now?

The minivan speeds forward as the highway dips down and banks left. In a moment it will rise up again as the Croton-Harmon Train Station comes into view off to her right. Exit now and try to lose them in the train station or the adjoining park? No, both will be desolate on a lazy Saturday afternoon. Call Chris? And tell him what, that his anxiety-ridden wife thinks a car is following her as she heads to the gym with the kids? No. No sense worrying him, and nothing he can do while working a case three thousand miles away in Los Angeles.

The road straightens out, bearing down as it crosses over the Croton River. The 9A/9 split is just a half a mile away. Left for Club Fit or right to improvise a new plan? She looks at the kids in the mirror. Good, they're oblivious, but what will keep them safe? Left or right? Right or left? She taps her fingers on the wheel frantically, then signals left, slowing down in the middle lane. The black car comes up on her quickly as she slows even more. She glimpses the driver, a white or Hispanic man wearing dark sunglasses and a plain, black ball cap. He tries to back off but the Passat has him wedged in. Michelle slows down to a crawl, forcing the black car even closer. The split is only a few hundred feet ahead. She accelerates hard, pulling away as she stays in the right of the two lanes going left.

C'mon, c'mon, stay close.

The black car takes the bait, accelerating and pulling into the left lane to give it some space. Michelle smiles, burying the accelerator. The black car does the same. At the split Michelle nails the brake hard, sending the Passat to within inches of her bumper. She cuts hard, exiting to the right, as the Passat exits left, forcing the black car on its left to do the same. Angry motorists honk and yell at Michelle as she smiles, relieved.

At least a mile before he can exit and backtrack to

find me. Michelle hits the iPhone, dialing her father-in-law, a retired NYPD detective. He picks up on the first ring.

"How's my favorite daughter-in-law doing?"

Michelle gathers herself for a moment.

"Hello? Michelle?"

"Just fine, Bill. How about a little impromptu visit with the kids?"

"Er, that sounds great. What time are you thinking?"

"About ten minutes. Meet you at the Marshalls in Arcadian?"

"Uh, sure... everything okay?"

"Never better, Bill. I'll see you soon. Bye." Michelle steps on the gas again as she passes by Mariandale, the Dominican Sisters' retreat center, determined to lose her stalker for good.

§

The man in the black car curses and bangs his hand against the steering wheel as the road curves up and away from Michelle Ravello. "Fuck! How could I be so stupid? Durand will have my head if I screw this up."

He makes a hard right onto Route 134 heading west, sending a spray of gravel toward the hot dog truck on the side of the road. A middle-aged customer jumps back and shakes his middle finger in anger as the driver stomps on the accelerator and flies through the residential neighborhood. Still time to catch up to her if he hurries.

§

Michelle Ravello weaves around heavy traffic on 9. She's just two miles from the Arcadian Shopping Center where she'll meet Bill Ravello. Small restaurants, a diner, car dealership, and a veterinary clinic fall away as she hustles through the area. *Just have to make it past the high school, then I'll be in the clear.*

Michelle hurtles through another traffic light, the kids squealing with delight as she accelerates along the steep decline. The van bottoms out at the north end of Aqueduct Street. Decades ago, in less politically correct times, this area was known as "guinea gulch" but is now home to a largely Hispanic population. The Ravellos sweep by the Ossining Bakery, momentum carrying them up the steep hill and through the traffic light at the intersection of Croton and South Highland Avenues. The large black and white clock tower, two more lights, and the high school lie just ahead. Michelle exhales, a big smile breaking across her face as she pulls up to the second set of lights, the high school just ahead and to her left.

§

The black car shoots past the Ossining Public Library and a string of stores that cater to the area's Hispanic population and comes to a screeching halt just short of the intersection of Croton Avenue and South Highland. The man grinds his teeth as he stares at the procession of cars ahead of him stopped at the light. He stomps his foot impatiently, leaning forward, ready to blare the horn as soon as the signal turns green.

And then it happens.

The blue minivan breezes through the intersection and travels up the hill just out of the man's view. A broad smile consumes his face. Moments later his light turns green, traffic splitting itself every which way as the man bears left and sees the minivan pulling away from the light up ahead.

Time to make you pay for the fucking stunt you pulled.

Clear sightlines allow the man in the black car to drift twenty car lengths behind the blue minivan. She outwitted him once today, but with greater stealth on his part, it won't happen again.

§

Her spirits buoyed by her impending meeting with Bill, Michelle drives on, oblivious to her stalker's reemergence. A Kentucky Fried Chicken, two gas stations, two banks, and a service station come and go as she arrives at the intersection of Rockledge Avenue and Albany Post Road. Michelle makes a right turn and a quick left, passing the CVS, McDonalds, Starbucks, and a slew of other stores in the strip mall. Thirty seconds pass before the black car replicates her moves. A minute later the man watches Michelle's car turn right and disappear beyond the Mattress Firm store at the far end of the strip. He parallels her path, turning right between two blocks of stores while still keeping his distance. Parking, he throws on a dark black coat and jogs forward. With only a supermarket and a discount store ahead, he's not worried about losing her again.

The man scours the Stop and Shop parking lot as he approaches. No signs of her or the car there. Must be by the Marshalls.

The stalker gives the department store a wide berth, finding a vantage point at the side of the supermarket, about a football field away. Within a few seconds he spots her. Gym bag in tow, feet covered with bright pink running shoes, she helps the children out of the vehicle. He studies the scene, pulls small binoculars out of his coat, and traces her path to the front of the store. The observer adjusts the dial on the binoculars, a thin smile forming as the image of Michelle hugging and kissing an older gentleman comes into sharp focus.

He peers at the scene as pleasantries are exchanged and Michelle kisses the children goodbye, waving to them as the trio pull away in the man's car. Michelle stands there pensively for a full minute, then her eyes dart nervously about, searching for his presence as he falls back into the shadows. Her examination of the area complete, Michelle ducks into Marshalls. The man creeps forward, keeping his eyes fixed on the department store entrance as he pulls a phone from his coat pocket. A wide grin engulfs his small face as the call connects. "All alone now. Want me to take her?"

▷ Chapter 2 ◁

Chris Ravello leans forward, staring into the hollowed-out corpse. The woman's chest cavity is a gaping hole with congealed blood pooled where her vital organs should be. Ravello scans the body. The victim is pretty and well dressed. Short, straight, strawberry-blonde hair crops an angelic face at peace with itself despite the blood splattered across it. She wears a dark red Halston dress, almost crimson, that flows to just above her knees.

Peering intently, Ravello studies the blood splayed across the dress. The splatter dies off as it approaches her bare skin. Beige panty hose and plain, black shoes complete her elegant outfit. She wears little makeup, a thin, gold necklace, and pearl earrings. There are no rings of any kind on her fingers, which, like the rest of her, enjoy an even, deep-brown tan.

Shards of bone, chunks of large vessels—most

likely her pulmonary artery and vein and her thoracic aorta—and clumps of blood are strewn about her upper body. She lies on the Los Angeles County Medical Examiner's stainless-steel autopsy table. A bloodied dinner napkin and dishwashing towel lay off to the side of her head.

FBI Special Agent RJ King fills Ravello in on the details: the body was found at the intersection of West 6th and South Flower Streets at 7:14 a.m. Bloody fingerprints had been scattered about the victim in an arc extending from her right chest, over her head, and down toward her left hip. The LAPD had the area cordoned off for the first few hours, long enough for the CSU to have gone over the crime scene and the coroner to have determined that death occurred between 2:00 and 4:00 a.m. that morning. Then the body was carefully moved to the morgue for processing.

Ravello rises up to his full height, eyes still fixated on the body. "Quite a mess, huh RJ? There's physical evidence all over the body and at the crime scene." He looks toward the special agent. "Even the FBI should be able to solve this one in no time at all, given the evidence." He shakes his head. "But the pattern of mutilation and sloppiness don't at all fit with Durand. What are we doing here? This should be the LAPD's case."

"You'd think so, but of course with Durand, nothing's that easy. There are no matches on DNA or prints in any criminal databases in this country, and none of it matches samples from Durand's lab. To add insult to injury, we can't even ID the victim."

"So what makes you think it is Durand?"

"This does, Yankee." King hands Ravello a note in a plastic evidence bag. As he reads it, his guts go into a free fall.

This changes everything.

§

Michelle stands in front of the store as she watches Bill, Christine, and James drive away. The knot in her stomach still pulled tight, her brain a mess, she stares off in the distance. With them out of harm's way, what now? Head over to Club Fit for a long run and the martial arts class as planned? Tackle some shopping for the kids? Stop by the police station and report the incident?

With pinpoint pupils Michelle searches her surroundings: just Saturday shoppers in search of a sale or two.

Then her eyes catch the movement.

Subtle. Off in the distance, cloaked by shadow, it would be easy to miss. But not for her. She smiles inwardly and ducks into the store with her gym bag. Catch me if you can, asshole.

Michelle makes a beeline to the back of the store and locks herself in the ladies' room. It takes her only a minute to peel off the running clothes and sneakers and don the beige blouse, sweater, and dark blue jeans. She pulls the hair tie out and straightens and adjusts her hair, then slips into the gray flats. The ladies' room door bangs behind her as she works her way through the store, grabbing a pair of large sunglasses and a full-length fall coat off the racks. She heads up to the checkout area, falling into line behind a gregarious-looking, large, black woman teeming with merchandise.

Michelle smiles at the woman. "Did a lot of damage today?"

"Oh yeah! Name brands for less for sure!" she says with a hearty laugh.

Michelle nods. "How's your hubby going to take it?"

The woman puts a hand on Michelle's forearm and cackles, "Girl, what he don't know, ain't gonna hurt him none." She turns to the cashier, who smiles as well. "Ain't that right, sister?"

"Amen to that," Michelle says. "Say, need any help dragging this to your car?"

The woman sizes Michelle up with suspicious eyes, then softens, "That'd be great, sugar." Those same eyes study Michelle's arms. "Didn't make much of a dent today, did you?"

"'Fraid not. Car got a flat on the way over and my husband's been on me to get the tires changed."

"Say no more, darling. Tell you what. You help me get this stuff to my car and I'll drop you off at the tire place by the CVS."

Michelle beams. "Oh thank you so much. I don't want to be any trouble...."

The woman jabs her in the side playfully with her elbow as they continue to checkout. "Ain't no trouble at all, deary." She winks. "We ladies don't stick together, our men'd be runnin' our lives in no time."

Bags filled to the gills, Michelle and her new-found friend head out the door, Michelle concealed by a multitude of shopping bags and the woman's generous frame. Michelle unburdens her arms in the back of the woman's SUV and then hops in the front passenger seat.

"I sure do appreciate this."

The woman smiles in reply as they drive off. A few minutes later Michelle hops out of the woman's car at the tire center and waves appreciatively as the woman drives off. "Thanks again."

The detective's wife smiles slyly as she jogs over to the nearby CVS, shopping bag in hand, ready to make full use of its vantage point. *Time to settle in for a little stakeout of my own.*

§

The figure glances at his watch, perturbed. Forty minutes. Must have seen thirty women come and go in that time. Muttering under his breath, he says, "Leave something for the rest of them, will you?"

He didn't have all day for this shit—okay, really he did, but that's beside the point. Hang here longer or press the issue? His feet answer for him as he nudges forward out of the shadows, pissed at dear Mrs. Ravello for inconveniencing him.

He parked behind the Marshalls earlier, a good move on his part. No exit out back meant she has to go in and out through the front door he's been casing. In and out with those frigging bright pink running shoes of hers. She might as well send up a flare when she's on the move! As the man approaches the store, he pulls up, waits for a few cars to pass by, and takes off the glasses and ball cap. He smooths his hair. Nonchalantly he looks around, then peers through a small opening in the store window not covered by one ad or another. His eyes dart left and right, then focus as far back as they can.

Nothing. *What the fuck?* They got a lounge or a beauty parlor in the back he doesn't know about? Grumbling, he approaches the door, tension starting to creep into his neck and chest. *Gonna kill this bitch when I find her, no matter what the boss says.*

The stalker enters the store and puts on a look of practiced boredom and apathy as he drifts about the aisles. Knick-knacks, candy, fucking hand-held board games. Who buys this shit? One hand holds his glasses and cap while the other rummages through everything. Slowly, methodically he canvasses the place, working his way to the back.

Gotta make sure she don't recognize me. He looks down at the cap and glasses, congratulating himself for his ability to blend in, change appearances at will. He stares at the glasses for what seems like an eternity, then blinks twice

Fuck, no!

The stalker moves briskly through the rest of the store, bumping into several shoppers along the way, offering his apologies as his insides ball up into knots: "Sorry, ladies." He holds a hand just short of his height. "You didn't see a woman about yay tall, black running outfit and pink sneakers?" The women look at him with disdain and hurry off. The man runs back to the restrooms, throws the door open to the ladies room. A woman shrieks. "Pervert! Help! Help!"

The man throws the glasses and cap back on and bolts out the door, a guard chasing him out of the store before giving up. He loops around to his car and tears the door open. Climbing in, he slams the wheel over and over with his hands and shakes his head side to side, spitting the words out, "You're a fucking dead woman!"

§

Michelle walks through the first set of sliding glass doors and leans against the wall of the CVS anteroom. She pulls off the gray flats, slips them in her shopping bag, and puts the socks and running shoes back on so she'll be ready to move quickly when the time is right. Pretending to look through her purse, shopping bag, and at her phone, she surveils the area, watching every car as it pulls out of the shopping center and drives away. There is a smaller exit to the strip mall, just down the road and out of her view, but she's not worried. Only locals living on or off Revolutionary Road or Rockledge Avenue come or go that way.

Michelle glances at her watch. Thirty minutes and no sign of him. Not exactly a rocket scientist. A parade of cars, SUVs, and trucks pull out of the shopping area and make their way north and south on Albany Post Road. Just when Michelle wonders if he'll ever catch on, she sees it.

The black car pulls up to the stop sign at the edge of the strip mall. Michelle backs farther away from the sliding doors as she takes in the scene. The doors whoosh open. An elderly couple looks at her oddly as they enter the store. The man in the black car spends an inordinate amount of time looking up and down the road as Michelle peers at him. *Hoping I'll just appear out of nowhere, idiot?*

The driver behind the man grows impatient, leaning on the horn, forcing him to move on. A quick right onto Rockledge and another right onto Albany Post Road and the car disappears from view. Michelle waits for a full minute, then two. If he's smart, up ahead he'll turn onto Revolutionary and circle back and try and catch me. Michelle smiles as four more minutes go by without the car reappearing.

She runs across the street, past the same set of stores she passed just an hour ago, and hops in her car. She's shaken one stalker today. Good for her.

But Michelle holds no illusions.

They must know where she lives. If their intent is to take her, they'll send multiple men next time. Men with better training. Men who won't stop until the job is done.

Pulling out her keys, her mind races through the options. Run? No, just delays the inevitable. Get local law enforcement involved? No way. Without proof they'd laugh her off as a scared housewife with an active imagination. Bring in the NYPD? Good option if Chris were around to pull some strings, but he's three thousand miles away. His partner and best friend, Detective Kevin Kennedy, would love to help, but thirty miles out of his jurisdiction, with no crime committed against her to date, there'd be little he could do to protect her. So it's settled.

She'll just have to go it alone.

Michelle turns the ignition key, firing up the minivan. She takes a few moments to run through the mental checklist of things she'll need for later.

Whoever said, 'Hell hath no fury like a woman scorned' never met Michelle Ravello, nor saw what she'd do to protect herself and her babies.

§

"You imbecile! One way in and out of the store and you let her escape? You fool!" The man takes an earful as he makes the right onto Rockledge Avenue while the idiot behind him blares his car horn. "Not sure how she slipped by. Maybe she—"

"Silence!" Heavy breathing on the line. "Where are you now?"

"Just pulling out of the shopping center."

"Good. Make a right at the light. At the top of the hill turn onto Revolutionary and follow it down behind the stores."

"Okay. What then?"

"Pull into the other entrance for the shopping center. The one by the back of the McDonalds and the dollar store."

"Okay. Gimme a sec... Yeah. See it up ahead."

"Park so the shrubs conceal your car but you've got a clear view of the other entrance."

"Got it. Almost there. Right, 'nother right. Okay, we're good," he says with cautious optimism. "Now what?"

"Pray to God she isn't already long gone. If she's still there and believes you've now left, she'll make her move in a few minutes and you'll tail her again."

"Smart, Boss."

Silence.

"Boss? Anything else?"

"Yes. Call me as soon as you spot her," then in an icy tone, "Fuck it up again and you won't live to see your own precious family ever again."

§

"Hi, sweetie. How's the shopping going?"

Michelle's casual tone belies her intense mood. "Oh, just fine, Bill. But still a ton more stops to go." She lets out a brief chuckle. "Say, if it's not too much trouble, would you mind keeping the kids overnight? It'll make it so much easier, faster for me. I'll get done in a day what would take me a week with the kids."

"Sleepover'd be great." His voice tinged with concern now. "Everything okay?"

"Just peachy, Bill. Thanks for asking." She starts to hang up, then adds, "Don't forget to get them to bed by eight. I'll call in the morning about what time I'll pick them up."

Bill starts to reply before realizing Michelle has hung up. He stares at the phone for a long moment, then shrugs before slipping it in his pocket. Turning to his grandkids, he makes a silly face. "Who's up for more ice cream?"

§

The observer's eyes stare straight ahead as

Michelle's blue minivan makes the two rights to pull back onto Albany Post Road heading south.

"I'm on her again, Boss."

"Keep me apprised." His sick laugh sends chills through the man. "Dear Mrs. Ravello fooled us once, but next time she won't be so lucky."

§

Michelle, her brain awash with a sea of thoughts and emotions, steers the minivan through heavy traffic along Route 119. As she heads east through the outskirts of White Plains, she smiles as she spots the large, white, Art Deco structure ahead. Looking like an old court house, The Westchester County Center hosts a staggering number of trade shows, seminars, concerts, and athletic events. Just over a year ago Chris and she brought the kids to a sweet Sesame Street performance there starring Elmo. Christine spent much of the performance spellbound and delighted before, much to brother James's disappointment, exhaustion gave way to her pleas to leave. Michelle's smile fades as she slows for the traffic signal and turns right onto Central Avenue, entering Westchester County's most densely packed retail space, a nearly ten mile stretch of stores that runs through four different municipalities.

As she passes the first of the massive strip malls, Michelle glances in her rearview mirror and notices the black car trying to be inconspicuous ten cars behind her. A small smile creeps onto her face as she gazes ahead and presses on.

Just after passing into Hartsdale, Michelle makes a right turn into a large strip mall and heads into a local pharmacy. There she picks up a few of the items she needs, pretending not to see her stalker as she checks out. Back in the car and several miles down the road, she crosses into Yonkers and makes a stop at a sporting goods store. She picks out an array of clothes to try on and heads into the ladies dressing room where she calls the front desk and asks them to put aside two items for her to pick up in a few minutes.

Michelle approaches the checkout girl, plopping the pile of clothes on the counter as she explains, "I called a little while ago about two other items. Could you add those to my order? My name is Michelle Ravello."

"Certainly. I'll get those for you right now, Ms. Ravello."

Michelle checks out, the two items buried in a sea of clothes.

§

Chris's eyes dart over the note again, looking for clues. "Is it real?"

"As far as we can tell, even though we can't find any of Durand's prints on it."

The detective turns the evidence bag over in his hands. The message is written in calligraphy on high-grade paper, giving it the look and feel of an invitation to a black-tie affair, perhaps a wedding.

A pity I've missed you again, Detective Ravello. Or perhaps it's you who've missed me. Either way, I'm sure we'll be getting reacquainted very soon... Sorry about the mess—I didn't have the time or inclination to clean up.

Hugs and kisses to Michelle...she's such a sweet, sweet girl.

Yours Truly,

Jean Louis Durand
a.k.a. The Giver

"I don't know what to make of this, RJ. Durand is taking credit for the murder, there are prints everywhere, but none of them are his?"

"That's about the size of it. Can't figure what the hell he's up to," King says with a scratch and shake of his head.

Ravello studies the note then peers over the body again, trying to piece it all together. Something's missing. But what? Was evidence removed or tampered with? Perhaps it's something more fundamental than evidence? He sighs. Despite working six months on the case, the detective clearly just doesn't understand what's going on.

"She doesn't seem pregnant and her abdomen is untouched," Chris says as he leans over the victim again. "We know this is about cloning and stem cell research, but what's his end game? And why has the pattern changed?"

"Ya got me, Yank. Twenty years with the Feds and I've never seen a case like this before. Just doesn't seem to add up. Maybe what we need is here, maybe it's not."

"We're missing something big, RJ... I just don't have a clue what it is."

$

Clouds blanket the sky and the moon. The cool, night air streams across the minivan as Michelle approaches the exit, her headlight beams cutting through the darkness on the unlit highway. She glances in her rearview, noting the black car a quarter mile back.

Tension creeps into Michelle's gut as she pulls up to the stop sign at the end of the exit ramp. A few more turns and she'll be home. Home but not safe, she fears.

The man traces her path, his desperate eyes locked on her vehicle as his hand searches in vain for the phone on the seat next to him. Fumbling with it, he knocks it on the floor. Cursing, he jams on the brakes, stopping short. The car behind him swerves, narrowly avoiding a collision. The other driver shakes his hand at the man and yells as he takes off. The man tentatively retrieves the phone, taking a few stuttering breaths as he dials his employer. "Just followed her off the South Street exit. Grab her at the house?"

"No, let her go."

The man's head snaps back. After all this time and effort? "Let her go? Uh, I thought I was—"

"You thought wrong," he snarls. "You've done enough for today."

The man's voice cracks before recovering. "Uh, sure... whatever you say, Boss." But his words are met with silence. He looks at the phone for a moment and shakes his head before turning his car away from the woman's minivan.

Michelle glances in the rearview mirror again. What the...? Turning off? Why?

The tension seeps into her upper arms and crawls up the back of her neck as Michelle approaches her home. Her eyes jump around, surveying the neighborhood. She drives past her house, looping around the neighborhood several times. No signs of him or anything out of the ordinary. Maybe I overreacted? Tailing her is one thing but making actual contact, attacking her, quite another. And for all his ineptitude in following her, the man had done everything possible today to avoid engaging her.

Michelle pulls into the driveway and dims her headlights, exhaling as she lets the car idle. As her eyes adjust to the reduced lighting, she studies the area once more, tracing every inch of the exterior of her house and the path that leads to it. All clear. She takes two deep, calming breaths as she reaches to turn off the ignition.

A loud clanging just ahead. Sudden movement. A metallic flash as he comes right at her....

§

After twenty fruitless minutes out at the crime scene, King and Ravello are agitated and annoyed as they ride toward FBI headquarters in King's Durango. What the hell is going on? Why couldn't either of them piece any of this together? Ravello is particularly upset, wondering if he's too emotionally invested in the case or just too stupid to figure out what Durand is up to?

"So, RJ, how'd the LAPD know to contact you so early on in the case? That crime scene was still fresh when you got the call and the Durand case has been quiet for months now."

"Well, truth be told, I've been sniffing around here the past few weeks."

"Why? All the murders up till now have been in New York."

"Well, that ain't exactly true, boy. I got word of two other Jane Doe murders in LA recently. Both involved strange patterns of mutilation. There was no note like this here case, but something about them smelled of Durand."

"What?"

"I can't put it into words. Just a gut feeling that bastard was involved. So here I am."

"I thought the FBI had left the Durand case for dead? Too much of a political hot potato and too few leads."

"Officially, that's true." King leans over toward Ravello. He speaks in just above a whisper, a rare thing for RJ King. "Between you and me—and I'll deny this from here to the Blue Mountains of Tennessee—something's not right about this case. The boys in Washington shouldn't have been so anxious to drop this one, so I'm not."

Ravello leans back and tips his head to RJ, acknowledging his respect for the risks King is taking in pressing on. "So what have ya got on the other two cases?"

"Same kind of victim profile as this here one: unattached, single white females. Not pregnant. No friends or family, at least none interested enough to step forward and identify them. He's adjusted his strategy." King shakes his head in frustration as he scowls. "Damn strange for a serial killer. They're always drawn to a type, and that's all there is to it. They go to town on them and ignore the rest. This one, he seems to be... picking and choosing. Whatever suits him at the time."

"Or fulfills his needs. Durand has been utilitarian right from the start. He's tried to make the murders seem like something else, but they've all been part of his greater plan. The murders are a means, not an end unto themselves."

"Okay. So what do we do now, Yankee?"

"Let's step on it and take a close look at the evidence on these last three Jane Does."

"Sounds like a plan," King says as he stomps on the gas pedal, throwing both of them back in their seats.

§

Frozen, she holds her breath and waits to see the inevitable weapon appear as the figure charges at her. But without warning, the figure suddenly veers off to the right. Michelle flips the headlights back on full force and sees the raccoon scurry toward a sewer. Straight ahead the lid to her silver garbage can rattles around before settling to the ground.

She buries her face in her hands, crying with relief as the fear and anxiety drains from her. Two minutes pass as she mentally collects herself, wipes at her eyes, and forcefully exhales. *Now that I've survived that false alarm and woken everyone in the neighborhood...*

Michelle cuts off the engine and the lights and surveys her surroundings, then turns her attention to the shopping bags next to her.

Over the next several minutes she deftly organizes the supplies according to her earlier plan. As she finishes up, she looks at the front door with trepidation, then with anger. Every day since her attack she has lived in fear, dreading what might come next.

No more.

Tonight she takes the first big step to reclaiming her life. She slips an object inside her bra, another in the back of her panties. Her face takes on a look of grim determination as she grabs her handbag, gym bag, and palms the nunchucks she picked up from the sporting goods store.

Tonight she takes the fight to them.

§

King and Ravello lumber along West 6th Street before taking a hard right onto South Bixel. They blow past the sprawling Good Samaritan Hospital campus and the low-rise buildings that dominate this part of the city. Moments later they screech to a halt inside the monstrosity that is the City of Los Angeles' FBI headquarters. It's 8:30 p.m. and pitch dark already, a testament to daytime's losing battle with the night as the year moves deeper into autumn.

King and Ravello take the stairs two at a time as they head up to the 3rd floor. Out of breath, they scramble over to the desk King commandeered for himself three weeks ago. Two other agents, neither of whom Ravello recognizes, nod to them as they settle in.

The detectives spend forty-five minutes combing through and discussing King's reports, more than enough time for the other agents to wrap up their business and silently head out the door.

They find little of interest.

As RJ promised, there are obvious similarities to the current Jane Doe case: sloppy crime scenes, lots of prints with no matches in any of the databases. The first Jane Doe had been skinned. Large strips of flesh were excised from her body. The second victim's body was untouched, aside from her complete, precise decapitation.

"There's nothing here to go on. Can you get me into the evidence room?"

"Does a bear shit in the woods, boy?"

Chris nods acknowledgment, laughing at RJ's lack of pretense. "Let's go, then." They ride the noisy, musty elevator down to the basement in silence.

RJ fiddles with the evidence room lock and then disappears for a few minutes with his FBI issue torch. King emerges with two bags of evidence, one per case. Chris helps him with the load as they make their way back to the creaky elevator and up to a conference room on the third floor. Gloved up they sort through it all, most of it clothes and the victims' jewelry. Nothing leaps out at either of them, despite Ravello's growing sense of déjà vu. He tries to dismiss the feeling as a case of hope meets desperation but finds he can't shake it.

Something in these bags calls out to Chris. But

what is it? There's no note from Durand, no memento that points to him. All they have are the clothes and jewelry the women had on when they died. A nondescript black halter-top, a red full-length skirt from Ann Taylor, a pair of jeans and a blouse, and some undergarments. All of it remarkably unremarkable clothes Ravello has seen Michelle wear herself every day since they had been dating. He scratches his head, wondering what he's missing? "What were the vitals on these two vics, RJ?"

Puzzled, he thinks for a moment. "Come to think of it, they were pretty similar. Numero uno was five foot six inches, a well-built hundred and twenty pounds. Victim two, if we assume a normal size and weighted head," he says with an irreverent laugh, "she would have been five foot seven and a hundred twenty-five. Why?"

"The last victim was about the same build too," Ravello says as he turns over a pink blouse in his hands. Something obvious is eluding him.

"What of it? He likes them tall and in good shape. So do I. You too for that matter, Chris. Michelle's about five foot seven, no?" King says nonchalantly. "There's plenty of women out there who fit this description."

"She's also about one twenty-five and has worn clothes just like this—recently," Chris says with increasing concern as he searches for the labels on the clothes. The hairs on the back of his neck stand up. SHIT! That confirms it!

"Who are you talking—"

"Damn it, it's her. It's Michelle!" Ravello thrusts the label of the black halter toward RJ. "See, a tiny 'MR' in black marker. One of Michelle's silly little habits. If you strain, you can just see it. See. She puts her initials on all her clothes. Says she dresses so much like every other woman, she needs a way to find her stuff if it's ever misplaced at the cleaners."

"Holy shit! That mother fucker."

Ravello's face turns ashen. "What'd the note say? Something about getting reacquainted soon, and hugs and kisses to Michelle, right?"

"Yeah, that's about what it said."

Ravello's jaw goes slack, his eyes blank, as the realization hits.

§

Michelle climbs the steps to the porch and silently slips into her home and locks the door behind her. Standing in the foyer, her senses are on heightened alert. Michelle's eyes look for motion, for anything out of place. Her ears strain against the silence for any sign she is not alone.

Nothing.

She turns back toward the door, leaning down to place her bags on the floor. As she rises up to flick on the light, a fist streaks through the air toward the side of her head....

§

Frantic, he dials the house phone, then her cell. No answer at either. Ravello redials both numbers. One. Two. Three times. They always kick over to voicemail.

Looking white as a ghost, Chris turns to RJ. "He's got her. Durand has Michelle, maybe the kids too! I need to get back there. Let's go!"

§

Michelle drops down, the fist flying through wisps of her hair as she thrusts her left leg out. Her foot finds flesh and bone, cracking two of her assailant's ribs as he collapses onto the floor in agony.

Sensing movement behind her, she shifts left too late. Powerful arms encircle her upper body, driving the breath from her. "Gotcha!" he yells in her ear. Michelle struggles to break free, striking his right knee-cap hard with her foot. Her attacker collapses, scream-ing in agony as he grabs his knee.

She flicks the house light on as the first man jabs at her, his fist connecting solidly with her left temple. She staggers back against the door, the nunchucks crashing to the ground. He presses his advantage, throwing a right cross at the center of her face. She ducks and pivots, his fist slamming into the door as she delivers a crushing blow to his groin. The attacker collapses to the ground like a bag of sand as his partner staggers to his feet.

As the second man hobbles forward on his good knee, Michelle jumps and kicks at his head. But he grabs her foot and lower leg and in a twisting motion throws her back against the door. Her shoulders and head slam into the structure, her body slumping to the floor. The man limps forward and then lunges headlong at her. Dazed, she manages to shift enough to make him just miss, his head and right hand bouncing off the door. His left hand juts out, grabbing the back of her hair as she tries to escape. He drags her, helpless, kicking and screaming, toward him. Her hands flail and scratch at the floor for traction, her right hand grabbing hold of a prized possession. Awkwardly, she pulls back from him, sending shooting pain throughout her head but halting her momentum just long enough to gather herself and then lunge backward. Twisting around, she drives the end of the nunchucks into the left side of his nose and left eye.

Blood spurts everywhere as he releases his grip and grabs at his face. Michelle scampers to her feet as his right hand disappears into his jacket, a gun appearing a moment later. With a quick flick of her wrist, Michelle sends one handle of the nunchuck into his right wrist, a grotesque crunching sound ringing out from the impact as the man screams again and drops the gun. Michelle fixates on the falling firearm, readying to grab it after it lands.

But two sounds freeze her where she stands.

$

Chris shoots out of King's Durango at LAX and bolts through the door toward the American Airlines counter. Blowing through security, he flashes his NYPD credentials and the FBI documents King gave him earlier and sprints toward the gate. Up ahead a long line at security awaits him. TSA does him a favor, processing him quickly, but won't go so far as to hold his flight, which is ready to depart in a few minutes.

"FBI! Hold that plane!" he yells while running the last twenty feet to the gate, waving his FBI ID. A stunned American Airlines representative stares at him, sizing up the situation while the gate door thuds shut.

"I'm sorry, Flight 846 has finished boarding," the worker says with remorse.

"This is official FBI business," he pants, trying to catch his breath.

"Are there terrorists on board?" the woman says with alarm as she picks the phone off the wall and eyes him with skepticism.

"I'm not at liberty to say. I need to be on that flight. I'm in pursuit of a serial killer."

She looks puzzled, unsure what to do.

"Look, I know this is all very bizarre and outside your normal training but look at my credentials. And please hold that flight at the gate so I can board."

The representative looks over his identification, as does the supervisor she calls over. They spend the next hour and a half—time Ravello does not have to waste—verifying his credentials and story and holding the flight.

At 11:33 p.m. Pacific Time the detective boards the flight amid angry glares from passengers trapped on the runway for almost two hours. He slips into his seat and ignores the stewardess's drone about oxygen masks and inflatable vests.

His family has their own emergency to deal with.

$

The first man's voice booms out, "Don't fucking move!" as he clicks off the safety on his own gun.

Michelle freezes, then slowly turns her eyes toward him.

"Looks like we got a fucking Bruce Lee wanna be," the man sneers, "eh, Rick?" He fishes a set of handcuffs out of his jacket, holding them up as he looks to his partner. "You got her covered?"

Blood all over his face, hands, shirt, and the hardwood floor, Rick grabs his gun with his left hand and eases himself onto his good knee as he huffs, "Yeah, I got it, Tone."

Tony inches his way over to Michelle, his gun trained on her chest. "Face down on the floor, toots."

She begrudgingly complies.

Tony secures her hands with the cuffs, then yanks at her. "Get the fuck up."

Michelle's mind races through her options as she staggers to her feet. Tony backs away and circles around to face her. "Try anything funny, I'll put one right between your eyes."

Michelle glares at him.

Tony barks, "Face forward against the wall, toots." He puts his gun away and pats down her backside, discovering a small knife in her panties. "Well, what do we have here?" he says with sarcasm as he holds it up for Rick to see. Grabbing her cuffed hands, he says, "Turn around, princess."

"Want me to take the front?" Rick says with a grin as he leers at her ample chest.

Tony throws him a disparaging look. "Mop up your frigging mess, hotshot. Husband's a cop. Don't wanna leave anything behind he can identify us with."

Rick heads off to find some paper towels while Tony carefully frisks Michelle's chest. Just as he's ready to move on, he discovers a second prize, a small can of pepper spray. He twists the object in his hand, admiring his discovery. "Figured you were slick, huh, get at least one by us?" His expression sours. "Just ain't your night, toots."

The glare again. "What the hell do you want with me, anyway?" she says, spitting the words at him.

Tony shrugs. "Above my pay grade, toots, but you can ask the boss yourself later."

Rick returns with a roll of paper towels and a garbage bag and starts sopping up the blood and hair. Tony nods his head. "Soon as he's done, we're outta here."

"I need my bag," she says.

"What the hell for?" Tony replies.

Michelle looks down at Rick, blood dripping from the paper towels, then back at Tony. "Feminine issues." She smiles. "Unless you want the back of your car to look like my floor."

Tony's face fills with disgust. "'Nough already." He walks over to the bags. "Which one?"

"Both." Skepticism fills Tony's face. Michelle starts to speak, "One's got pads, the other tam—" He puts up a stop sign as he picks up both. "Where's the friggin' bathroom?"

Michelle leads the way. Once there, Tony cases the small bathroom and stretches the bags toward her before he reconsiders, dumping them on the bathroom counter. He sifts through the contents, grabbing her old flip-style cell phone, a nail file and clipper, and a few stray bobby pins. Smiling, he says, "No need for these, toots." He moves to pass her. "Have fun in there." But she steps in front of him, jerking her head toward her wrists. "Can't take care of business with my hands behind my back."

Tony nods apathetically, pulling out his gun before he removes the cuffs. He cocks the hammer. "I'll be right outside."

Tony slams the door shut and stands guard as Michelle locks the door. Running the water, she opens up the cabinet under the sink and rifles through it, finding the small bottle of cleaner she uses to get soapy buildup off the tub. She repeats the process with the linen closet and places another item into her bag. Not enough, but it'll have to do. Going back to the cabinet, she dumps out a few small baggies she keeps make-up supplies in and fills the bags with tampons and pads. Crumbling up the boxes, she takes an applicator from one of the tampons and packaging from one of the pads and fills up the small trash can next to the toilet.

Ten minutes later Rick and Michelle have both finished cleaning up. She comes out of the bathroom and hands Tony the bags, holding her wrists out for him. He looks at her with mild surprise, then cuffs her and tosses the bags in the hallway. He starts to go, but Michelle's eyes bore a hole through him. "Might want to take those. Just started today." Tony looks at her with annoyance and grabs the bags as he yells to Rick, "Let's get the hell out of here before Miss Feminine Hygiene needs any other shit."

⊳ Chapter 3 ⊲

Jean Louis Durand—a.k.a. The Giver—smiles as he rubs his cheek against Michelle's. She pulls back and spits at him as her wrists strain against the cuffs. "Get away from me, you pig!"

The sociopath holds a hand to his chest. Feigning offense, he says, "Your words cut me to the core my dear, sweet Michelle." He shakes his head, then reaches out and runs his fingers along the scar on her neck and snickers, "Hopefully you'll find this visit less painful than the last."

"What do you want, Durand? Running out of other women to terrorize?"

The sociopath casts her a lecherous look, then runs his eyes all over her while he nods in appreciation.

"Torture device. Insurance policy. Leash and crop for dear Christopher. All rolled into one pleasing package." He turns to his men. "Bring her to the lab so she can see what we have in store for her and her dear husband."

§

Chris Ravello brings the Firebird to a screeching halt in the driveway next to Michelle's minivan and shoots across their small porch. He fumbles with the keys for what seems like an eternity before barging through the door and into the foyer. As he scans the stairs ahead of him and the living room and dining room to his right and left, everything appears to be in order.

Powering up the stairs, his ears are on alert for any sounds or movement in the house. There are none. He glances at his watch: 9:06 a.m. Everyone might still be sleeping on a Sunday morning. He turns right at the top of the staircase and goes in the kids' rooms, Christine's first, then James's.

Both are empty. The beds are still made. The detective spends a minute or so in each room playing crazed dad, looking under the bed, in the closet and drawers, hoping to find his children hidden away.

Nothing.

He runs down the plush, white-carpeted hallway, past photos of the four of them at a picnic at Untermeyer Park and others of an afternoon of croquet at Dad's house. He throws open the door to the master bedroom, praying Michelle will shriek.

She doesn't.

Their room, like the kids', is untouched. Pristine.

Over the next few minutes he reins in his emotions as the scared, concerned father and husband melts away and the cold-hearted, logical detective in him takes over. He calls around to Dad and Michelle's friends. He leaves messages and hears the same speech numerous times: "Sorry, Chris, I don't know where Michelle and the kids are. Is there anything I can do to help?"

His phone rings. It's Dad. "Everything okay, Chris?" he says excitedly. "I was in the shower when you called."

"It's about Michelle and the kids...."

"You want to speak with them?"

"Huh... who?"

"The kids. I'm just getting Christine up."

"Thank God they're all right." Ravello feels like an idiot for not considering the possibility everyone stayed at Dad's. He hadn't even tried to call him from LA before racing back here like a lunatic. "Sounds pretty silly, but I didn't see anyone here and I got worried. Can you put Michelle on?"

"She's not here. She dropped the kids off yesterday and called back last night to ask if a sleepover would be all right; said she was running late with errands and had a bunch more to do today. Where are you? Didn't she tell you?"

"I'm at the house; just got back from LA. Michelle's not here, though the minivan is. The bed hasn't been slept in or the shower used and none of her friends know where she is."

"That's strange. Not like Michelle at all."

"I'm gonna try her cell again. You okay with the kids a few more hours?"

"Sure, Chris, do what you have to do."

"I'll update you later. Bye."

Chris speed dials Michelle and gets voicemail again. Michelle has been acting strange at times since the attack, but this is unprecedented. Has she taken off? Was she abducted? A million scenarios race through the detective's mind.

$

The CSU combs through the house. Kennedy brought them in as a favor to Chris. Later they'd explain why a Peekskill missing-persons case required the NYPD. For now they just need answers.

Two officers work on the minivan, dusting for prints and collecting fibers. Three other CSUs canvass the house, as they've been doing for the last hour.

"We'll find her, Chris," Kennedy says solemnly and with determination as he stares straight ahead at the house.

Ravello shakes his head, disgusted at the turn of events. He did what needed to be done, responding to the crime scene in LA. Nobody could have foreseen this. Kennedy's gaze shifts to him. "Don't beat yourself up, Chris. There's nothing you could have done differently. And besides, the murders in LA have turned up what we've been looking for: fresh leads on Durand."

"Yeah, and all I needed to do was turn Michelle over to him to get those leads."

"You really think Durand did this?"

"He must have. There's Michelle's clothes on the first two LA victims and the taunting note from him on the third. But how'd he get back here in time to kidnap Michelle after the last murder? Does he have someone working with him now?"

Kennedy puts his hand on his friend's shoulder. "We're gonna get her back, Chris. Whatever it takes, we'll get Michelle back."

Chris looks directly into Kennedy's eyes, wanting desperately to believe him, to believe in the power of his words. "I hope you're right, my friend," he says limply.

§

A thin smile creeps along The Giver's face as he sits in his office and stares at the computer printouts. Crow's feet radiate from his outer lids as his pale blue eyes, cold and hard, crackle with energy and interest. The results confirm it: Durand's work is hurtling forward at breakneck speed. Playing off of and against Ravello brings out the best in him. Sure, there had been that little run-in in Midtown, but that was his fault, not Ravello's. He had become sloppy, overconfident, an occupational hazard when you are a sociopathic mad scientist with an IQ of 173. The smile spreads clear across Durand's face.

The Giver sees the big picture clearly, how both Ravellos are integral to achieving his plans. Theirs is an epic tale, one with far reaching consequences for everyone who calls earth their home. Durand will savor the days and weeks to come, what they mean for his work, for mankind—for dear Christopher and Michelle Ravello.

Durand rises and quickly exits his office. It's his custom to check on the lab several times daily and today he will share it with his newest guest and plaything—Michelle Ravello. He strides down the hall, past several offices of his underlings, and enters his security code onto the keypad outside the door of his lab. The Giver passes through the sliding glass doors as they part before him.

The first area is where harvested cells from victims are turned into multicellular clones. Centrifuges, micropipettes, flasks, test tubes, and a slew of chemical compounds highlight Area One. As spectacular and impressive as Area One is, it pales in comparison to what is being accomplished in the rest of the facility.

Durand has no interest at the moment in Area One. He wants to be where the action is. He moves deeper into the lab.

Areas Two through Four are a production line—for human beings!

In Area Two, the multicellular clones are bombarded with serums that cause their maturation into fetuses, babies, and ultimately toddlers. A vast array of incubators, the initial ones immersed in a compound that mimics amniotic fluid, guide the clones through the process. In the latter stages of Area Two, feeding occurs entirely via IV tubing that supplies all the necessary nutrients for the developing clones. Goosebumps fight for space on Durand's arms, and the hairs on the back of his neck stand at attention as he works his way through Area Two. So much time, effort, and money have been expended to make his dreams into a reality.

Area Three is where the most explosive growth takes place. As such, it is the most testing intensive area in the facility. EEG machines, stress test equipment, including vials of radioactive tracer substances, and electromyography devices abound. Here a clone's heart rate, lung capacity, cardiovascular output, brain wave, and muscle function are constantly analyzed and adjusted for peak performance. Clones are grown into their mid-twenties in Area Three.

Durand keeps his gaze forward as he marches through Area Three.

Area Four is "finishing school" for the clones. A clone's age is adjusted as necessary, and the chemical bombardment of the clone's brain is concluded. Who the clone is and its mission are imprinted into the clone's cerebral cortex in Area Four. They are injected with nanometer sized devices. These devices are programmed to adhere to blood vessels and nerves throughout a clone's central nervous system and to the heart and other vital organs. These tiny devices ensure the clone's complete and utter obedience to Durand.

Area Four is the most fascinating and fearsome area in the facility. It is comprised of twelve separate operating room suites. Within each suite is a cart that contains long vertical cylinders. Small balls, ready to dance up and down in the cylinders, rest at the base. Masks, tubing, and drawer after drawer of meds round out each cart. In the center of each room a massive, movable lightsource springs from the ceiling and stares down on an adjustable bed. Implantation of the control devices takes place in these rooms under carefully controlled circumstances.

Durand has repeatedly warned his lab manager about securing Area Four at all costs. He will do so again now. If a clone escapes Area Four before processing is complete, it's possible for it to act entirely upon its own volition—nobody in Area Four wants to learn what that would mean.

Durand smiles as he looks around. The entire facility is state-of-the-art, beyond state-of-the-art, really. Everything is a prototype, surpassing equipment available at similar facilities in the way the modern-day race cars surpass Ford's first Model Ts.

The lab manager, Thomas O'Toole, double-times it over to Durand. He knows his Boss has an infallible memory, no tolerance for misdeeds or a misspoken word, and little patience.

"The plant is working out very well, sir. We've moved past the slow start and technical difficulties that plagued us earlier. We're at peak efficiency now."

"Excellent. You are to be commended for your efforts, Tom. Just don't lose sight of quality. We're not striving for a production plant of mindless clones like in an Aldous Huxley novel. No, each clone takes a great deal of time, effort, and money. Each must be perfect in every way."

"I understand, sir. Great care is being taken to live up to the full breadth and depth of your vision. Any product with even the slightest flaw is destroyed, and the process begun anew."

"Good. When will we have the next one in place?"

"A week, ten days tops. We'll stay right on sched-ule... unless someone like Ravello interferes again. Should I be concerned about that possibility, sir?"

The Giver's laugh sends a chill up and down O'Toole's spine. "Not unless frequent flyer miles can harm us. I'll have Ravello scurrying from one coast to the other, desperately trying to figure out what I have planned for the world at large and him in particular."

"You just love torturing the detective, don't you, sir?"

"Since my near apprehension, I have stepped up my surveillance of Detective Ravello and my analysis of his areas of weakness. One such weakness will be joining us shortly," he says with a smile. "Soon I will have the dear detective begin his walk with us on the dark side," The Giver says with another throaty, bone-chilling laugh, "and I'll be sure he has some unexpected companionship on his journey."

§

The moment CSU finishes, Ravello jumps in the minivan and heads over to his dad's. His world crashing down all around him, he needs the unconditional love only his family can offer to help him keep it together and relieve the stress. Traveling south on Route 9, the Welcher Avenue exit just ahead, a call comes in from Kennedy.

"We got prints back on the house and minivan. One of them matches those at the warehouse where you were shot at."

"Great, Kev. That was fast. I'm surprised that case and this one are connected."

"You're going to be even more surprised now, Chris.... The print also matches Michelle's. Her prints, along with the kids', are on file with the Greenburgh Police Department."

"What! How can that be? And how does Greenburgh have prints?" he says, incredulous. Ravello feels a stabbing pain in his chest that radiates to his left arm.

"Last fall Michelle had photos and prints of herself and the kids taken at Hillside Park in Elmsford. It helps the police track kids who are abducted. Greenburgh PD sponsors the day every year, tying it into one of their child safety-seat checks at the park."

The pain is building, like a vise now. Chris gasps for breath. The timing on his latest attack couldn't be worse. He forces the words out, "Got it... but how the hell... did Michelle's prints show up at the warehouse? Makes no sense...."

The pain is searing. He needs to pull over somewhere.

"I know, but CSU triple checked. There's no mistake," Kennedy says warily. "You okay, bud? You don't sound so good."

The road goes in and out of focus. He blinks hard to keep from smashing into something and steers toward the side of the road, hoping he doesn't lose control. "I'm fine, man. Thanks."

Blackness follows.

§

"Ah, Mrs. Ravello. So glad you could join us," Durand's voice dripping with sarcasm. Michelle looks around Area One speechless, impressed by the sophisticated equipment and endless array of chemical compounds.

Durand turns to the guards who brought Michelle to him. "Leave us now."

The guards exchange a look of puzzlement, then head to the exit. One of them punches a security code into the pad that opens the door for their departure.

Durand provides a quick overview of the area, going into greater detail as Michelle shows a surprising interest in his methods.

A short, stout lackey comes over to Durand as he's addressing one of Michelle's questions. Annoyed at the intrusion, he asks, "What is it, Carl?"

"Sorry, sir. Might we speak in private for a moment?" the underling says amid fidgety hands.

Durand rolls his eyes. "Make it fast," then turns to Michelle. "Try not to get in too much trouble while I'm gone."

The two men walk briskly away to the far end of Area One.

Their backs to her, Michelle sneaks over to a workbench. She scrutinizes the labeled test tubes, looking for the right combination, then smiles.

These will do nicely.

Glancing toward Durand and Carl, engrossed in conversation, Michelle reaches for two partially filled test tubes. The sound of approaching footsteps freezes her. She drops down, slipping under an opening in the bench. The footsteps grow louder, seemingly right on top of her, as her eyes grow wide. Arms folded over her bent knees, she holds her breath, praying she's not discovered. Suddenly, the foot falls drop off in intensity, then fade away. Michelle exhales forcefully and thanks God before leaning forward for a look.

All clear. Now for the test tubes.

More footsteps. She turns her head skyward in frustration. *Really? You've got to be kidding!*

§

Carl makes steady eye contact with Durand, resisting his urge to look away from the sociopath. "Our source tells us Detective Ravello just arrived back home. The CSU and his partner are canvassing the residence—and the minivan—for clues to his wife's disappearance."

Durand smiles. "And so it begins. Have Tony and Rick meet me in Area Four in fifteen minutes." He places a hand on his worker's shoulder. "Good work, Carl," he says before dispensing with him and marching back toward Michelle.

Michelle turns toward the bench, one hand batting hair from her eyes as she runs the other admiringly along one of the centrifuges.

The Giver stops his march and casts her a disapproving look. "It's hardly a blender, Mrs. Ravello."

She offers an embarrassed look as she removes her

hand from the machine. "Sorry. Brings me back to my undergrad days."

Durand raises a skeptical eyebrow. "Failed pre-med student?"

"No, just a chem major. Thought about cancer research until Chris got into med school...." Her voice trails off.

Durand folds his arms in annoyance. "How droll." Then with extreme sarcasm, adds, "Perhaps we can share more another time." He grabs her arm and yanks her toward him. "Come now."

$

Coming to, Chris's clothes are soaked with sweat, and he has cuts on his right cheek and jaw and large patches of red around his right eye. His upper eyelid is swollen, making the vision in his right eye fuzzy. He turns his head an exaggerated amount to the right so he can see things out of his left eye.

The front passenger's side of the van is badly damaged from where he'd hit the guardrail, but the rest of the van seems intact. The pain in his chest is all but gone.

He scans the area; fortunately, no one is around, but he knows state troopers will be there soon. Backing the van away from the guardrail, he takes off on 9 again and makes an illegal U-turn to head north, knowing he's in no shape to see the kids or Dad or answer anyone's questions right now.

The phone rings somewhere at his feet. He kicks around to try to find it, the van lurching and jerking as he comes off and on the gas and brake. It's RJ.

"Any new developments in the Durand case, red-neck?" he says with false bravado.

"'Fraid not, Yankee. How about on your end?"

King and Chris had spoken just after he discovered Michelle was missing. All he needed now was an update. "This one will blow your mind. They found prints at our house and in Michelle's minivan that matched the warehouse in Brooklyn."

"Great. Whose is it?"

"Michelle's."

There's an awkward silence.

"Come again? Did you say it was Michelle's?"

"That's right. Can you believe it?"

"Honestly? No way, no how. Maybe it was planted."

"It could be, though I don't know how they'd get Michelle's prints to begin with. So there's nothing new on your end?"

"No, 'fraid not. Say, what database were Michelle's prints in?"

"A local one. Greenburgh PD had them from a 'fingerprint the kids' event they held last year. James, Christine, and Michelle had their prints taken and IDs made up to assist in tracking the kids in case either was ever abducted. Never thought it would help in finding Michelle.

"You can contact Arnie Fertig at Greenburgh PD, 914-555-1287, to have a look at the prints. The ones from the warehouse are in IAFIS."

"Fertig at Greenburgh PD, you say? Gimme a minute, Chris." RJ's voice becomes faint as he leans away from the phone and barks orders. His pursuit of Durand, vis-à-vis Michelle has just become official FBI business again. About six minutes later he comes back on the line. "It's an uphill battle here with these dumbass local yokels, but I've got the Bureau on it. Don't worry, Chris, we'll find Michelle. I've also got a couple of agents from NYC going over to your pappy's to assist with protecting the kiddies."

"Thanks, RJ. I know what a pain in the ass the bureaucracy is at the bureau. I appreciate you protecting my kids while I'm off hunting down Durand."

As he drives home, King and Ravello spend the next fifteen minutes trying to figure out what Durand is up to. Did Michelle tie into the murders or was taking her just a way for Durand to torture them both? How had her prints appeared at the warehouse? Was it more Durand trickery or had Michelle somehow been drawn into all of this? She's been acting strange since the attack. Maybe it's more than post-traumatic stress disorder?

Why had Durand's MO changed? A careful and

precise pregnant lady and baby killer before, he was now a sloppy and careless murderer of young, unattached women. Is he becoming impulsive and irrational, entering a phase that will soon lead to his arrest? Or is he carrying out the next steps in a master plan they had yet to figure out?

They don't have any meaningful clues connecting the disparate crimes—until RJ is interrupted by one of the agents he spoke to earlier.

Their voices are muffled but clearer and louder than before. Chris can make out parts of the conversation.

"What? You certain, boy? Makes even less sense than before, now... Shit. All right."

Ravello yells through the phone. "What's going on, RJ? Any new evidence is good evidence as far as I'm concerned."

King returns to the phone. "Got a feeling you're going to eat your words, boy."

"What the hell are you talking about?"

"The prints at the last murder scene out here—they're Michelle's too."

§

Michelle Ravello peers into one of the twelve operating room suites in Area Four as Durand talks excitedly about his research. "...where we implant the technology. Care for a closer look?"

"S... sure. Why not?"

Durand flashes his hand across a sensor, the door springing open before them. "After you."

Michelle tentatively enters, looking around at the gleaming structures and instruments with a combination of amazement and fear. She's no expert on ORs, having been in one only twice when she delivered her babies, but this one looks light years beyond most in its sophistication.

As Durand rambles on about nanotechnology, controlling his clones, and delusions of grandeur, Michelle casts furtive looks at the anesthesia cart. During her time as a pharmaceutical rep, she called on many different kinds of doctors, including pain specialists, most of whom were anesthesiologists by trade.

May be something there I can use.

Michelle nods at Durand, offering the appearance of interest while she navigates toward the cart. A handful of syringes, each dutifully labeled, sits atop the structure. She leans her backside against it, her right hand drifting behind her back as she distracts Durand by pointing to a long, shiny gun across the room. "What is that?"

Her fingers crawl along the cart, over one syringe, then another.

"Our implantation injector for the nanometer control devices." He picks it up.

Almost there.

"We place it over the clone's forearm or neck and..."

Her thumb and pointer finger wrap around her prize and drag it toward her.

The OR door flashes open, startling Michelle. Jumping, she lets go of the syringe as Tony enters first. Rick, favoring his right knee, with bandages adorning his wrist and nose, follows. Both men scowl at her before turning to Durand. "You wanted to see us, Boss?"

Durand's face becomes cold and calculating. He turns to Michelle. "Yes. Let's show her what we have in store for dear Christopher."

§

Chris's brain is a cross between the deep dark nothingness of space and the jumbled static of a TV on the fritz. Unable to process this latest development, he says nothing.

"You still there, Chris?"

In just above a whisper he replies, "Yeah, I'm here. Durand must have planted those prints too. Up until my trip to LA, I'd spent every day with Michelle. She hasn't been anywhere near LA in the recent past." Downtrodden, he continues, "It's got to be a setup to get me out there again." He pauses, stalling for time to think. "Well, I'll play along to see what he's up to. I'm almost home. Let me get a quick shower and grab a change of clothes and wrap some things up with Kennedy. I'll be on the first flight I can get out of LaGuardia."

"Will do. I'll meet you at the airport. Call if you need anything."

The detective lets the phone slip out of his hand and fall into his shirt pocket.

They are both drained and badly in need of recharging, but there's no time for that now.

§

Michelle stares in disbelief.

An exact replica of her!

Her eyes dart between the clone and Durand. "When? How?"

The Giver laughs, relishing her confusion. "You really need to be more careful about who you trust with your dry cleaning." His laugh dies down, a smile filling his face. "A few stray hairs were more than enough to get us started. Not to mention the clothes themselves." The laugh again. "What a nice touch that was, playing dress up with our latest victims in LA."

Anger lights up her face. "You put my clothes on your corpses? You sick bastard!"

Durand folds his arms over his chest. Coolly, he says, "And planted your prints."

She shakes her head in disbelief. "Why go to all that trouble?"

A thin smile curls across Durand's face. "For your dear husband's benefit, of course. We kidnap you while he's on a wild goose chase out in Los Angeles, then leave him clues so he can race back panicked and grief-stricken." The laugh returns. "Warms my heart to torture him so."

Michelle lunges forward, her right hand hurtling through the air on a collision course with Durand's face until Tony stops it in midair. He twists the arm behind her and yanks her head back by her hair as Michelle cries out in pain.

"Got a live one here, Boss."

"Indeed we do," Durand says with admiration. His cold eyes pierce hers. "But it's all for naught, my dear. We will torture your dear husband mercilessly, dangling you for bait. And in the end, after his depravity has reached its Zenith in the name of saving you, we'll have him join forces with us."

Tony tightens his grip as Michelle screams, "You're a dead man, Durand!"

The Giver steps forward, runs a hand along the left side of her face as she struggles to break free. "On the contrary, my dear. Your death is what will make all of this possible."

He looks to Tony. "You have preparations to make. Lock this one away and get to it."

MICHELLE'S CAPTIVITY 2

JOURNEY TO THE DARK SIDE

▷ Chapter 1 ◁

Durand leans back in his office chair, the phone pressed to his ear as he waits for the call to go through to his West Coast assistant, a Beverly Hills plastic surgeon. "Richardo. Yes, yes doing quite well." He shakes his head, bored with the pleasantries they are exchanging. "Yes, your contributions have been invaluable in advancing my work." Durand stares at his desk, at the series of eight-by-ten-inch close-up photos taken of Chris Ravello during the LA investigation. His left hand slowly uncovers one photo after the next as a sick smile emerges.

"I have two more jobs for you, so listen carefully. My instructions need to be followed to the letter...."

§

Tony shoves Michelle Ravello across the tiny makeshift room, watching her stumble before tripping on the cot and slamming into the wall. "Have a nice fucking night, toots."

She spins around and charges the door, reaching it as it slams shut in her face and the lock is engaged. She tries looking through the peephole but realizes this one looks into the room, not out.

Michelle surveys her surroundings. A small cot. A sink, toilet, and a small table. A glorified prison cell minus the steel bars. She smiles as she spots her handbag and gym bag lying in the corner.

They stopped her from taking the chemicals and drugs earlier, but she has plenty of other tricks up her sleeve.

She grabs the two bags and sits on the cot, using her body to shield what she's doing from the peephole. Grabbing one of the running shoes, she peels out its sole, lifts out her smartphone, and powers it on. The partially eaten fruit icon appears. Punching in her passcode she looks at the phone and frowns. Barely any battery life left and no way to charge it. She quickly navigates through her recent calls, finds several from Chris, and hits callback, hoping she can say everything she needs to before the phone runs out of juice.

$

Ravello takes Peekskill's South Street exit and a

few twists and turns later pulls up next to the Firebird. As he's getting out of the van, Mozart's "A Little Night Music" pierces the air. He has only assigned one person that ringtone—Michelle.

"Chris, help me! He's got me. I'm in…"

"Where are you honey? Are you all right? Michelle?"

"I'm not sure, I think I'm—" The phone goes dead.

"Michelle? Michelle!" He tries returning the call, but it won't go through, kicking over to voicemail instead.

For the second time today the detective fumbles with his house keys, resisting the urge to kick the front door in instead. He's tired, strung tight, and struggling to think clearly. Was Michelle somewhere nearby? Should he stay local and scour the area? If so, does he trust the NYPD enough to help him? Or would the suspected mole in the department mean the NYPD is more of a hindrance than a help to him?

In the end, he decides to stick with his original plan, so he showers, dresses, and takes off for the airport, this time in the Firebird. The call with Michelle was so short and inconclusive he has to just ignore it and plow ahead.

As he heads through the Bronx toward LaGuardia, Ravello puts in a call to Kennedy, who confirms he has Chris's back and that FBI agents are watching over Ravello's family as promised.

Chris shakes his head as he exits his car at the airport. It's so hard with this investigation to know what the next move should be and his gut tells him many more lives—including Michelle's—now hang in the balance.

◊ Chapter 2 ◊

nother day, another body missing and/or dead. That disturbing pattern is all too familiar to them. Overnight, LA time, Durand claimed another victim. Another 'Any idea what I'm up to? Catch me if you can' murder. This time the victim is a young, white male with the stage name John Adair, murdered in the outskirts of LA.

Murder victims' bodies are usually cleared out quite soon after the CSU and ME finish their work at the scene. But progress was slow on these Durand murders, so RJ requested the LAPD leave the scene intact a few hours longer for them, in the hopes they would make some kind of breakthrough by analyzing the body at the scene.

Ravello crouches over the lifeless, naked body, searching for answers. Why does the victim profile keep changing? Is there a link to Michelle aside from her prints once again appearing at the scene? Why is Durand playing head games with them, him in particular? Does it get him off or is Ravello somehow part of his plan? That last thought is as scary as it is bizarre.

The body is mutilated, just like the rest. Like the last few, the pattern of the mutilation keeps changing. The left part of John Adair's face is missing. The skin and muscles are gone, leaving an intact skull in their place. Adair looks like a gruesome comic book villain, a cross between Spawn and Two-Face. His right deltoid, right middle finger, and right leg from the knee down are also gone. Who knows what the hell Durand is up to?

Still crouched over, Ravello peers up at King. "Guy doesn't ever seem to rest, huh?"

King looks at him impassively as he reaches into his sports jacket. The sound of his cell phone surprises them both, redirecting his hand. "King here," he says with that perfect mixture of apathy and anger only the best in law enforcement can conjure up. "Un-huh. Yeah. Yeah. NO shit? Have it analyzed top to bottom, inside and out, before we get there. Ought to be by early this afternoon at the latest. Good work."

King pulls the evidence bag with the note in it out of his pocket while Ravello looks at him with anticipation.

"'Nother Durand job, just north of here. Take a

look at this here note. It was propped up over pretty boy's genitalia before you got here."

Ravello looks over the note. It's identical in style and presentation to Durand's earlier one:

My, my, how the mighty have fallen! What is that saying? 'They have ears but they do not hear, eyes, but they cannot see.' Hope your other senses are working better, Detective. You'll need them...

Give my best to Michelle when—if—you see her again.

Untruly Yours,

Jean Louis Durand

The detective hands the note back to King without comment.

"Any details on the latest vic—"

King's phone interrupts them again with its "Sweet Home Alabama" ringtone. That melody is forever seared into Chris's soul. A vivid reminder of one of the worst moments of his life.

The call is from Kennedy. Chris had forgotten to turn on his phone after the flight.

Michelle is dead.

§

The door to Michelle's room flies open, Durand marching into the cramped space as his men wait outside. A look of mock concern fills his face as he shakes his head. "Tsk, tsk. Poor, poor Christopher. Races back out to LA to investigate another grisly murder... only to be summoned back home by terribly upsetting news."

Michelle scowls at him, spitting out the words, "What have you done this time?"

"Killed you," he says with a smile.

Michelle's head snaps back, her shoulders slumping as her face collapses. "Oh no." She bows her head, her eyes tearing up. "Oh Chris."

Michelle stares at the floor for a long time, then turns her eyes to Durand, her own twisted smile emerging. "He'll never believe it's me."

Durand reaches a hand toward her face, aiming to amplify her despair with an unwanted caress. She swats the hand away and glares at him. Cocking his arm to strike her, he reconsiders. Emotional pain will inflict much more damage right now than his hand ever could. "And why is that, my dear?"

"All your sophistication and planning, and you miss something so basic?"

His eyebrows arch.

Her hand goes to her neck, tracing his handiwork from months earlier. "The scar on the clone's neck looks different than mine. Chris will pick right up on that."

Durand nods with appreciation, impressed by her acumen. He measures his words. "Anyone but you and he would. But his incredible grief, the disturbing way we mutilated the clone's abdomen, our 'something old, something new, something borrowed, and something blue' motif. All these things will distract him from the truth." The Giver looks at her with pity. "The note we left him, the fact your dear husband has no idea we are using clones, these things will convince him the corpse is yours."

Michelle stares at him, unblinking. Heart breaking, mind reeling, she takes a deep breath, then two as she struggles to process it.

The Giver looks at her, a feeling of deep satisfaction growing, spreading through him. He turns to go, intent on leaving her to wallow in her grief.

"So why do it?"

He halts. "Excuse me?"

"Why leave an imperfect scar? Why rely on theatrics in the hope Chris doesn't figure things out?"

The tiniest glimpse of uncertainty appears on his face before he banishes it.

Michelle, excited, points at his face as she laughs. "You couldn't do it, could you?" She smiles. "The all-powerful Dr. Durand with all your state-of-the-art technology and delusions of grandeur and you couldn't do it." Her hand traces the scar again. The words come faster now. "Cloning me from a single hair, aging the clone decades in a matter of weeks or months, that you could do, but aging a jagged cut a few months, having the scar appear just right, that's beyond you." Her eyes twinkle as she smugly smiles at him.

His own eyes are two seething orbs. His hatred spills over, reaching out to strangle the life from her.

Michelle presses her face right up to his. "Not so all-powerful, after all."

He coils his arm again, wanting to lash out, but feeling impotent to do so. His lips begin to move but there is nothing to say. A long, long moment passes, their eyes locked in battle. He leans back ever so slightly, his eyes turning away first. He casts her a brief look, then Durand departs without another word, the door slamming shut behind him.

Filled with grief and a spark of anticipation, Michelle stares at the door, hoping she's a step closer to walking through it a free woman.

§

The Feds and the NYPD swarm over and about the house with spotlights, spilling into the backyard where just a few hours earlier Michelle was strung out on the old hammock he had yet to pack away for the impending winter.

Ravello is a cauldron of conflicting emotions: immeasurable grief, anger, guilt, and remorse doing battle, tearing him up inside.

Kennedy had gone with him to identify Michelle's body at the morgue. There, he could see she had been mutilated like the first of Durand's victims, her abdomen torn apart while the rest of her was left unscathed. Her face had the blank stare of death. Her telltale radiance, always a beacon in his life, was completely extinguished. Her soft, flowing hair crowned her beautiful face and held a single red rose near her left ear when her body was discovered. An involuntary smile crossed Chris's face when he noticed among her things that Michelle wore the pearl earrings he had gotten for her last birthday.

At the crime scene Michelle had also worn a tight white blouse and dark miniskirt. Her arms were posed provocatively about her, one in an arc extending over her head, the other with the hand resting on her hip.

Tears welled in the corners of Chris's eyes when he saw the bracelet he gave Michelle during their courtship. Photos from earlier showed Michelle wearing a small blue ribbon that extended from the belt loop of her skirt. Her left knee was bent, draped over her right knee. Her legs were clean-shaven and unscathed and she wore a pair of gray Reebok walking shoes. Like the ribbon, they were unfamiliar to the detective and seemed out of place.

In the backyard at the house, Kennedy hovers around his friend, uncertain what he should do.

"You going to make it, Chris?"

"I don't have much choice, do I?..." Ravello's voice

trails off. He is frozen. Just as the note foretold, his eyes and ears are useless right now. They are gathering information, but none of it registers in the least. "There was another note?" he says cautiously.

"Yeah." Kennedy turns and yells to a CSU member. "Roberts. Bring a copy of the note over here. Now."

Roberts looks up from collecting dirt samples. He puts the last of the samples in a small glass jar, closes the top, and slips it into a case that contains leaves, hairs, and fibers. A short jog later he is beside them, pulling a copy of the note out of another case he carries.

Roberts is a frail, prematurely balding fellow in his mid-twenties with a small ring of rust-colored hair. He is as well regarded on the force as he is painfully shy. "Uh, here you go, detectives," Roberts says as he extends the note toward them and averts his eyes. "A preliminary analysis of the note at the lab shows no prints except the deceased's. According to our FBI sources, the note is identical in style to the ones found in LA."

"Thanks, Ken," Kennedy says as Roberts stands still, quivers, then scurries off.

Ravello's eyes fixate on the note.

My Dearest Detective Ravello,

It seems we have finally come full circle. Beginnings and endings have merged into one. Prophesies and vows have been both foretold and fulfilled. Ah, but there is still much that remains for you and me to share. Grieve as you must, but do not dawdle.

Many lives depend on you—and me.

Your Friend & Confidante

JLD

Chris's whole body goes numb as he finishes the letter. A few minutes pass before the full weight of Michelle's death and the Durand predicament sink in.

His beloved is gone forever, killed by a madman he couldn't capture.

⊳ **Chapter 3** ⊲

Durand, Michelle, Tony, and Rick stand at the top of the large hill. Her mouth gagged, hands tied behind her back, tears rolling down her cheeks, Michelle finds herself unable to turn away from the scene unfolding far below.

A cool, stiff breeze blows through the autumn air. Fall-colored leaves—brown, orange, yellow, and red in hue—crackle with the last vestiges of summer. Chris's black hair tussles about as he stands with a downcast expression on the rolling hills of Gate of Heaven Cemetery in Hawthorne, New York. The funeral mass ended about an hour ago at Church of the Magdalene in nearby Pocantico Hills. It was a lovely mass at the quaint, little country church the Ravellos frequent. The last bit of dirt is tossed on Michelle's casket and Deacon John, Bill Ravello, the kids, and almost everyone else has begun listlessly moving toward their cars. Chris feels as empty and alone as he ever has.

Kevin Kennedy and RJ King stand opposite Ravello. Each man is wise beyond their years in the ways of tragedy and death. Each is also ignorant when it comes to consoling a friend and brother about his loss. Minutes drag by in silence and separation, each of them feeling the enormity of eternity swirling around and suffocating them.

Police Commissioner Kelly breaks up the pathos. Decked out in a dark blue suit and conservative tie, he offers condolences. "Terribly sorry for your loss, Chris. Michelle's death shakes each of us greatly. She was the salt of the earth," the Commissioner says with a resigned shake of his head.

"Thanks Commissioner," Ravello says sullenly. "I for one won't rest until Durand pays for his sins."

Kelly's head pulls back. Ravello can tell what he just said didn't sit well with the Commissioner. Kelly reaches his hand out to the side of his officer's shoulder.

"Rest assured, Detective... Chris. We'll search high and far to find a more definite link back to Durand. And when we do, we'll pounce."

The detective feels the restraint in him collapse. A river of emotion pours forth.

"A more definite link? With all due respect, sir, what are you looking for? A friggin' videotape of Durand murdering Michelle?" Chris shakes his head, enraged.

"Michelle would still be alive if the NYPD didn't hold me back since her first attack." Ravello knows Kelly had stood in Chris's way, impeded his progress. He just doesn't know why.

Kennedy jumps between Kelly and Ravello and pins his hands to his friend's shoulders, looking at Chris like a trainer does with his woozy fighter during a title match. "Let's have a minute to chill out, to cool down, eh, Chris?"

"It's okay, Detective Kennedy. I've said what I need to." Kelly turns and fades off into the distance.

Chris stares into and through Kennedy's eyes. "I'm going to nail that bastard Durand, and anyone on our side of the fence working with him. Heaven help whoever that may be."

Silent up to this point, RJ chimes in. "Amen to that, brother. We've got your tail."

"That's right, Chris. No need to look beyond us three for the answers," Kennedy continues.

With the clarity that comes only from all consuming rage, Ravello hears Kennedy's message loud and clear, and knows his friend is right.

The answers lay right in front of him and have all along.

Durand turns to Michelle and smiles wickedly. "Now you see the truth, my dear. Your husband, his friend Kennedy, the entire NYPD, none of them will be looking for you anymore." Durand looks far down the hill at the grave, savoring the moment, then turns back to her. Running a hand across her face as she struggles to pull away, he smiles. "Any hopes you had of escaping are buried with her now."

§

Michelle leans against the door in her room, ear pressed against the hard wood, straining to make out what they are saying.

The last week since her confrontation with Durand has been a complete let down. At the funeral the other day, Chris showed no signs of realizing the clone wasn't her. And who could blame him? Adult clones whipped up in short order from a wisp of hair? She wouldn't have believed it herself if she hadn't seen it with her own eyes. But all the disappointment, heartache, and let down are behind her. It's all on her shoulders to find a way out of here, and she needs to make it happen fast. Everyone thinks she's already dead. What's there to stop Durand and crew from making that a reality?

"...finally starting to piece it all together," Durand says.

"How so, Boss?"

"He just learned some of the prints at the LA murders are from my earlier victims."

Michelle hears Durand's muffled cackle through the door, imagines the sick look on his pompous face.

"Through Detective Kennedy they've also learned we were stealing plastic surgery supplies at the warehouse in Brooklyn."

"Ain't you worried about them closing in on us?"

Michelle's eyes narrow in concentration.

Durand laughs again. "Hardly. Couldn't have drawn up the plan any better."

Michelle's hands ball up into fists, flexing open and closed. *Just give me a few minutes alone with that bastard...*

"At long last they've connected the stolen plastic surgery supplies to our West Coast operations and brought poor Dr. Viejo in for questioning. As we speak, Special Agent King and Ravello are questioning one of the dear doctor's patients, the supermodel Holly Williams." Durand cackles. "Seems she was quite unhappy with the plastic surgeon's latest efforts on her behalf and filed a complaint with the LAPD that ultimately got King and Ravello involved in the case." Footsteps closing in on the door. Michelle lingers as long as she can. "Now the real fun...." She bolts over to the cot and settles in, assuming a look of boredom as the lock and then the door tumbles open.

Durand nods to Tony, who grabs Michelle as Durand whips out his phone, making the call that will change all of their lives forever.

$

Renowned supermodel Holly Williams sits across from Detective Ravello at a desk in RJ King's office. Questioning her for the last twenty minutes, he's come up with nothing of interest. "So Viejo never mentioned a Doctor Durand as far as you can remember?"

"No, not that I remember, Detective. Sorry," replies the tall, black English model with the sculpted body, her eyes offering an apology.

"Okay, Miss Williams, well thank you for—"

Ravello's phone rings, coming up "restricted." He grabs the call.

"Good day, Detective. I see you found one of my little helpers. Do be cordial with him, and please don't harm him—you know how I detest violence."

Ravello stands when he hears the voice, unsure of who he's talking to. "Durand?"

"In the flesh!" After a brief blood-curdling laugh, Durand continues, "Any idea what to make of all those fingerprints that are turning up?"

The detective is fuming, livid through and through. "You're enjoying yourself, Durand, very pleased with your games, I'm sure."

"Of course, dear Doctor Detective. But let us not drift off topic. Perhaps a familiar voice will jolt you to recognition, help you put the pieces together."

"Chris, are you all right? Are the kids all right?"

A lightning bolt shoots through him. "Michelle? How is it possible? Is it really you?" He fumbles along.

"You're dead... we just buried you. Told the kids..." His voice trails off. Holly casts him a perplexed, yet sympathetic look.

"I'm alive, Chris. Durand is using clones to—"

"Michelle! Michelle!" he screams.

"Visiting hours are over for now, Detective. I'll leave it to you to piece together the clues. Do it quickly though. We're moving on to a new phase, a New Order if you will, and I've saved a place just for you, Detective. So if you have any intention of ever seeing your dear Michelle again, you'll do just as I say.

"Now, let's talk about your assignment and the partnership I'd like you to forge with the lovely super-model you're interviewing...."

⊳ Chapter 4 ⊲

Manhattan's 17th Precinct

Detective Jenkins stands before him. A lanky, thirty-six-year-old misfit with a bad case of acne, his career and Chris's diverged long ago. He leans his backside on the corner of a desk across from Ravello's and hunches his shoulders forward and to the right, as if trying to stretch his back out from yet another poor night's sleep. It's long past most everyone's bedtime now: 2:30 a.m. to be exact.

"Sorry to hear about Michelle," Jenkins laments. "Must be tough."

"You don't know the half of it," Ravello says with a solemn shake of the head as he rises to his full height. "Here, walk with me a bit, then you've gotta get back home to Bonnie. No late-night carousing for you tonight." Ravello waves Jenkins in as they reach the elevator, then hits the button for the first floor.

"I hear ya, Chris. Been better since I started going to meetings twice a week. Still... a couple of hours at Empire City and a beer or two at Rory McFlynns would hit the spot."

Chris looks at Jenkins with disapproval as the elevator stops its descent and its doors open. "Why don't you count your blessings, Carl? Your wife's still alive, you've got two nice kids, and you're just twelve years from retirement. Don't blow it by falling off the wagon." Chris waves him off.

"Yeah, ma... ma... maybe you're right," he stutters. "Let's rain check it on the beer," he says as he slinks off through the front door of the precinct. Chris looks left and right then descends the stairs to the evidence cage, in disbelief about what he's about to do.

It takes him just three minutes to get in and out of the cage, Durand's evidence stuffed underneath his shirt and an old plaid sports jacket, as he heads out to the Firebird. To her credit Holly is wide-awake. Either that or she's sleep-flirting.

"How'd it go, sweetheart?" she says with fluttering lashes as she leans her cleavage toward him.

"Piece of cake, and in a twisted way kinda fun," he laughs, his nonchalance belying how completely torn apart he is about what he's just done. "Maybe I've been on the wrong side of the law enforcement thing all along." Holly looks a little stunned but then laughs it off.

"Don't know about that, but you might as well dive right in and make the best of it, huh, luv?" She leans even closer, slipping a hand onto his upper thigh. "No telling where all this could lead."

Chris shoos her away as he dials Durand on a Nokia, prepaid, throw-away phone he provided. "Mission accomplished. But why didn't you have your NYPD or FBI moles get the stuff for you? Seems it would have been a lot easier."

"Ah, yes. But so much less fun than having you do it. Besides, who can I trust more, someone on both my and the NYPD's payroll or the husband of the woman I'll kill if he slips up?"

"Point taken," Ravello says through gritted teeth. "So when do I see that beloved wife of mine?"

"Not so fast, Detective. There's something else I need you two to take care of first. I'll be in touch."

A dial tone drones in Chris's ear, Durand's way of reminding him who's calling all the shots.

And so begins the young detective's life of crime.

§

"Ah, the things we do for love," Durand says, his voice filled with sarcasm as he smiles affectionately at Michelle. "Just two days ago your dear husband was hell-bent on bringing me to justice to avenge your death." He laughs heartily. "Now he's committing crimes on my behalf in a desperate attempt to free you."

Michelle glowers at Durand as she sits across from him at his desk, her hands bound together with rope as Tony stands by.

"I must say, Christopher dove right into his assignments." The Giver sneers at her. "Perhaps it's the company he's keeping."

"What the hell are you talking about, Durand?" Michelle demands.

He arches his eyebrows in mock ignorance. "Oh, you don't know?" He leans forward. "His partner in crime is none other than Holly Williams."

"The supermodel?" Michelle asks with confusion.

"One and the same," Durand replies with glee. "And they are working very closely together." He looks to Tony. "Correct me if I'm wrong, but she's become quite smitten with Detective Ravello, hasn't she?"

Tony nods and with a low-pitched laugh adds, "And the bitch is used to getting whatever man she wants."

Durand juts back, a hand on his chest, feigning surprise. "But surely she wouldn't seduce a married man, asking him to betray the sanctity of his vows."

Tony offers a slithering smile. "From what I hear Williams gets off on that kinda thing."

Michelle stews in her anger, then lashes out. "You don't know my husband. He'd never—"

"Never what, my dear?" Durand asks. "Never steal evidence for a sadistic serial killer? Never cavort with a slutty, house-wrecking supermodel while pretending he's doing it for his dear wife?" Durand thrusts his head back and laughs deeply. "Perhaps it's you who don't know your husband, Mrs. Ravello."

Michelle grinds her teeth to dust, her blood lust toward Durand palpable.

Durand laughs for a full twenty seconds more before settling down, his face growing more serious as he stares at Michelle with intensity. "What depravity we have in store for dear Christopher and Ms. Williams." He shakes his head. "Mark my words, my dear. Soon you'll want nothing to do with that degenerate husband of yours."

§

Package Express Warehouse, Lower Manhattan

"There is no way you can come in, Holly. It's too dangerous, and you're too inexperienced. You'll get us both arrested. Just stay in the car and be prepared to bolt out of here."

"I'm far from inexperienced, Chris. You should be so lucky to find that out someday, luv," Williams says with an inviting smile as she adjusts her white micro-miniskirt and tight red top. "You heard what Durand said. He wants me with you every step of the way— otherwise he'll kill Michelle. I guess the bugger's got some warped Bonnie and Clyde stuff lined up for us."

"Well, 'Bonnie,' you're staying in the car on this one. Between the miniskirt and the heels, we'd have no chance of getting out of there alive."

"True. But, can you think of anyone you'd rather be trapped in a building with?" Holly says with a wicked smirk.

A smile breaks through to the surface as Chris struggles to maintain his composure. Holly is as intoxicating and distracting a woman as he's ever come across. "Funny, very funny, but let's look alive out here. I oughta be out in ten, fifteen minutes, tops," he says as he slips out of the car and closes the door, turning away before she can ensnare him.

Ravello scurries through the early morning darkness and finds the loading dock area, the center's weak link security-wise. His heart is pounding as he sweats profusely. He makes a much better cop than criminal, he muses as he leans against the brick wall and takes a few slow, deep breaths before plunging inside. Thirty seconds later he's in the locker room donning a Package Express uniform when Ravello faces his first challenge.

"You a new guy?" the lumbering, shaggy-haired worker says as he emerges from a nearby bathroom stall. He extends his hand in greeting to Chris, a hand he has yet to wash since coming out of the stall. "Joe Oliver."

No time to second guess how to play this.

"Chris Meloni. Nice to meet you, Joe," Ravello says as he reaches out against his hygienic better judgment and shakes hands. Before Oliver knows what hits him, Ravello pulls him forward, sucker punches him in the jaw, and throws him, out cold, onto the floor. Shit, might have overreacted a tad bit on that one, he thinks as he shakes the pain out of his hand and figures out what to do next.

Ravello hears footsteps but can't tell if they are coming toward him or passing by the locker room. He grabs Oliver, drags his fatness back into the stall, and locks it before sliding out along the floor. The footsteps recede as they pass the locker room entrance. Whew; too close for comfort on that one.

After a couple of more deep breaths, Chris exits the locker room, hugs the wall, and a few twists and turns later finds himself in the main warehouse. It's a humongous structure that makes your local Costco seem like a mouse hole. Despite it being very early in the morning, workers buzz about, some on foot, some operating forklifts or other machinery, all engrossed in their activities. It takes a few seconds before the detective orients himself to his surroundings, the layout being a perfect match with the blueprints he memorized before the job.

The most vulnerable part of the task is coming up next. Ravello strolls across a thirty-foot expanse in the center of the floor, feeling like every set of eyes in the place is on him. He guesses none in fact are, as he meets no resistance in ascending a metal ladder secured to the wall. One floor up, he follows a perforated metal catwalk to the area of interest, "perishables." The packages, cooled on the inside by dry ice, nonetheless feel like any other Package Express packages he has ever come across. He checks tracking numbers and hoists three of them on his shoulders. Easier than expected.

"Need a hand?" bellows a short, stocky guy from the next aisle. Chris mumbles a "No, I've got it" and makes his way back along the catwalk toward the ladder, his heart thumping against his chest. There's no way to go down the ladder with three packages in tow, so he veers off toward the elevator next to it.

"Here, let me get the door for you," the annoyingly helpful coworker offers. "First time at Manhattan, Downtown?" he says as Ravello walks past him into the elevator. Is the man studying him, questioning who Ravello is or just a helpful guy? The detective braces his arms, ready to pounce on him at the slightest provocation.

"There, you're all set," he says as the door closes between them and the elevator descends. Despite the coolness of the warehouse—it can't be more than 65 degrees Fahrenheit—sweat beads on Chris's forehead and collects in his armpits. Just a little longer and he'll be out to the car....

As the elevator door opens, Chris finds himself face-to-face with two Package Express supervisors, both clad with the characteristic blue and white emblazoned shirts. Hard hats obscure their ears and eyes and cups of Starbucks Coffee fill their faces. Chris veers off to the right, judiciously avoiding any contact whatsoever. Much easier than expected—until he spots Joe Oliver down the hall, speaking with a guy who also appears to be a supervisor. Oliver points at him, starts yelling, "That's him! That's him."

Ravello quickens his pace.

The calling out becomes louder, more forceful. "Hey, you. Stop! What do you think you're doing?" Just ten feet from the loading dock he hears footsteps stampeding toward him.

Ravello makes a break for it, charging through the dock, the packages held tight in both arms.

His running back days at Fordham University flash before his eyes. He careens off of two burly loading dock workers who must have played ball themselves, second string he's sure. A third plants himself in Chris's path, his massive arms flexing at his sides. The look on his face says he won't be denied. Ravello head fakes left, then breaks right. The worker doesn't flinch. Instead, his arms encircle the detective's waist and yanks him down.

Ravello improvises, sending the corner of one package into the other man's left eye. He curses and recoils as Ravello does a spin move, continuing to run as he peels himself off while executing a 360-degree turn. The edge of the dock is rushing up toward him. He takes an awkward mini-leap in mid-stride—one that would have obliterated him back at Rose Hill—and lands half on his feet, half on his side. One package shoots forward.

Bodies began flying off the dock at the detective as he races forward. Holly has the Hummer idling twenty feet ahead, just inside the chain link fence whose door is sliding closed. The rear passenger door flies open just as he dives for it. Holly peels away, door still open, Chris's body and the packages jangling about. They blow through the fence, unhinging it from its track and cable system.

Chris pulls the door shut and hurdles into the front passenger seat. "Nice work, Bonnie. Head west on North Moore Street, and then we'll switch cars in the garage before we take the Westside Highway up toward the Henry Hudson. We'll be out of the city in no time."

"Nice work yourself, Clyde," Holly says with a provocative grin and a glance toward the detective before she returns her attention to the road.

"Step on it," Chris says. "We're not out of the woods yet."

§

"This is the only other clone we have of Michelle Ravello?" The Giver asks as he looks down at the woman strapped onto the OR table. Her chest rises and falls in rhythmic fashion as her body lies immobilized due to the effects of general anesthesia.

Tom O'Toole nods. "Yes, sir. Would you like me to begin work on another?"

An anesthetist and two nurses, clothed in scrubs, look on.

Durand looks over the naked body carefully, admiring its beauty and perfection. He shakes his head. "No. We won't need another after this one." The Giver's soulless blue eyes stare at the clone's delicate, unscathed neck. "Just two final preparations to make." He nods toward his OR team. "As you inject the nanometer technology, I'll harvest a small area of skin from elsewhere on her body and fashion a scar on her neck."

Durand's eyes shine in anticipation as a thin smile spreads across his face. "It won't be an exact replica of Mrs. Ravello's scar, but it will be more than sufficient to fool her dear husband given the circumstances he'll be seeing her under."

The Giver turns back to his team as he settles in next to the body. "Let us begin."

▷ Chapter 5 ◁

The Giver and Michelle sit at the small conference room table in a specially designed sound-proof room. Ahead of them two closed circuit TV monitors, dutifully recording any and all movements in the adjacent hallway and the two rooms off of it.

"You're crazy if you think you'll fool him again," Michelle says with conviction.

"You underestimate the incredible strain your dear husband has been under these last two weeks. He's lost you once already. He doesn't want to go through it again." Durand rubs his hand along his chin as he stares back at her. "Christopher's eyes will see whatever his mind needs to keep his hope alive."

They turn to the monitors, Rick and Tony marching Chris down the hallway.

Ravello's head is awash with a sea of emotions,

reeling from the crazy things he's done, the risks he's taken in cooperating with Durand. A few weeks ago he complained when some of Durand's evidence went missing at the precinct. Three days ago he stole vital evidence for the serial killer from the precinct! The next day he was nearly taken down by three Package Express workers as he robbed their warehouse. Ravello knows he can't continue to press his luck. He needs to find a way to free Michelle before he's caught, fired, imprisoned, or maybe killed. For now he bides his time, ready to pounce if he senses an opportunity.

Chris walks down a long hallway, a blindfold and iPod masking his senses as Durand's men guide him along.

Inside a small, dark room with a closed circuit TV monitor, Durand's men free him. There he converses over the monitor with a woman he believes is Michelle. It seems to be her; she says all the right things and looks the part in the flowery pastel dress the detective gave her last Mother's Day. But without being able to touch her, how can he be sure? Too few things are as they seem these last few months.

"You see, my dear, he hasn't a clue," Durand chortles.

Michelle shakes her head as she pleads at the monitor. "Just take a good look, baby. Please."

Durand smiles slyly as he enjoys the theatrics. A few minutes into it, Tony enters the room to watch over the real Michelle as Durand slips out the door.

Chris speaks to Michelle with enthusiasm, but keeps his heart hidden from view as he studies her over the monitor. The mannerisms are Michelle's, yet somehow different. Forced? Rehearsed? Maybe just Michelle bending under the pressure of the last five months? It's impossible to tell through a TV. He needs her touch to know.

After just four minutes, Michelle and Chris are shepherded away from each other as Chris is brought face-to-face with his sociopath nemesis.

"Enjoy your visit with your beloved, Detective?" Durand says in earnest. "More will follow if you continue to cooperate. Perhaps we'll even throw in a conjugal visit to keep your spirits up," he says with a cackle.

"In all seriousness, you have surprised me this last week, Detective. I expected begrudging obedience. Instead, you've approached your work with enthusiasm and professionalism. We may yet lure you to the dark side." Durand's smile fades. "One more challenge—an altogether formidable one—lies ahead. This final task will require some female assistance. Steer your way through it unscathed and we will kiss and make up.

"But remember, no funny business. Your dear wife's life hangs in the balance."

Michelle stares at the monitor, fighting back tears as she takes in the scene with Chris and Durand. Her head slumps forward into her hands as the realization hits; the only hope either of them has right now is a false hope.

▷ Chapter 6 ◁

"**Y**our husband's journey to the dark side is near complete, my dear."

Michelle shakes her head, scoffing at the serial killer. "You wish."

"And to think you are the reason it's all possible. His desperation to see you, to save you, means he'll do anything I ask, including betraying your trust."

Michelle slams her hand on the conference room table, then jumps up and jabs angrily at Durand. Tony moves to intercede, but The Giver puts up the stop sign.

"You'll never get away with this, Durand. And all I saw through those monitors of yours was a heartbroken, noble man who'd do anything to save his wife." Michelle waves her hands in the air. "Whatever you think you see, they're the delusions of a sick, sick man." She stares at Tony, daring him to take her on so she can kick his ass again. A minute goes by, Tony standing his ground but nothing more. Michelle drops back into her chair with a huff and folds her arms.

Durand rises up, leaning across the table toward her and spits out the words. "Your knight in shining armor will be at a sex party tonight with Holly Williams, re-cruiting my next victims." He offers her a contemptuous smile. "My, my, what perverse activities lie ahead for dear Christopher this evening. And we'll give you a ringside seat for much of it."

$

Melville, NY

Semi-naked bodies abound. A swatch of fabric here or there to cover a loin or breast or ass. The place is a sea of carnal desire. Tonight's theme is Rome meets Sodom and Gomorrah, Ravello guesses. Women with heaving breasts and gold-leafed hair adornments min-gle with men with fig leaf crowns and tight spaghetti strap sandals. Chris is far, far out of his element and for once is glad to have Holly with him. She moves with ease and surprising anonymity. Maybe the tight fitting, skimpy toga is enough of a change of context to throw the swingers off—maybe no one cares who they are screwing this evening. It's almost Halloween, for Christ's sake, maybe that's helping this supermodel to go undetected in plain sight.

Chris acts casual, relaxed, one arm draped over Holly's shoulders, the other pumping a Bacardi Rum and coke to and from his mouth. But clothed in a light tunic and on the prowl for new victims for Durand, he is exposed on every level and can't let go of the thought: Spatick and Commissioner Kelly will crucify him if they get wind of what he's up to.

Their hosts, jovial, masked, and effervescent, have spared no expense. Sand, palm trees, and mood music create a Carnival atmosphere. At five hundred dollars a couple, with about three hundred in attendance, they can be more than generous in setting the proper mood. There is much kissing and fondling as couples, threesomes, and quartets drift off to the bedrooms that outline the large playroom they are mingling in.

It's now 11:30 p.m. Holly and Chris have already talked it up with twelve people, none of them fitting Durand's explicit physical and psychological profiles. They're in between encounters now, trying hard to be inconspicuous—easier said than done for a cop and a supermodel. Holly relishes the opportunity to run her hands all over the detective and whisper in his ear.

"Bet you never had this kind of fun with Michelle, huh, luv? Out in LA this is considered a G-rated Saturday night for me."

Chris stays silent, uncertain how to react to the come-on. He needs to play his part if they're going to pull this off. But he also needs to maintain discipline and self-control around Holly. It's a battle he feels destined to lose.

"I really appreciate your help on this, Holly. There's no way I could have gotten into this party without you, and I know you're risking a lot to help me get Michelle back."

"Come on, baby, you've got to loosen up before you give us away," Holly says with her sexy British accent as she leans into him, grabbing his buttocks, slithering her tongue in his mouth. He responds in kind, then runs a hand over her tunic and reaches in and cups her left breast. Holly doesn't flinch. On the contrary, she gyrates her hips and slides her mouth next to his ear. "It's about time you showed me some attention, Christopher. I was beginning to think you'd never come under my spell." She nibbles on his ear, caressing it with her mouth and tongue, then slides back in front of him, her face radiating warmth and sensuality. Her eyes lock in on Chris's as she draws him—body, mind, and soul—in to her. "Play your cards right, Ravello, and you're in for an unforgettable night."

Holly leans back as an equally horny couple approaches. He's tall, toned, with leading-man looks and a bulge in his tunic. She's five foot four, svelte, and exotic looking: Asian-Philippine or perhaps Hawaiian. Finally, two people who fit Durand's descriptions.

Holly and Chris exchange a knowing glance. Then they dispense with introductions and small talk and head toward an unoccupied bedroom "guarded" on each side by musclemen dressed as Eunuchs. Their friends go in first, followed by a couple they haven't seen before. Holly holds Chris back for a moment at the door.

"Prepare, Detective, to have your world rocked to its very core." With that she pushes him into the pleasure room—obliterating life as he has known it.

◆ Chapter 7 ◆

Tony and Rick drag Michelle along, her hands bound in front of her. Reaching their boss's office, they stuff her into a chair across from him as they await further orders.

Durand looks into her downtrodden eyes, beginning his monologue. "At long last we'll complete dear Christopher's transformation." His eyes shine. "Anything to say before we give you a bird's eye view?"

Michelle stares back at him listlessly, her lips remaining still.

"Very well then." He waves to Tony and Rick. "Bring her to my chambers. I need to make the last of my preparations." He smiles as the men grab Michelle and lead her out. "Time for a little misdirection and amusement."

The Giver picks up his office phone and dials

security. Time to put the clone in place. "Fetch Michelle Ravello for me at once. I'll meet you at the security office."

§

Two guards lead the woman they think is the real Michelle toward the security office at The Giver's facility. They push her through the door and into a small room. Inside, one wall is filled with closed circuit televisions that monitor every square inch of the facility. An adjacent wall holds racks of guns, ammunition, handcuffs, knives, walkie-talkies, and Taser guns. Straight ahead stands Jean Louis Durand.

The Giver plays his part, delighting in seeing his plan unfolding. "Michelle, we are approaching a seminal moment for your dear husband, Christopher, and I wanted you to have the best seat in the house for it." With that he grabs her and pushes her down in a chair that faces the monitors, before turning to the guards on each side of her. "She's in your capable hands now," he says. "See to it that she enjoys the show."

Durand opens the door and as he exits says, "I'm off to play ringmaster. Try not to miss me too much."

§

Tony and Rick stand guard over the real Michelle

Ravello, seated in Durand's private chambers. A wall of monitors before her guarantees a complete view of what is about to transpire. Michelle's head hangs limply, staring at the floor.

Tony grabs her hair and pulls it back, forcing her to look straight ahead. "Boss said he wants you to see it all, no matter what."

§

The six revelers spill out of their chauffeured stretch limo, laughing, kissing, and groping as their chaperones guide them—still blindfolded—into the compound. Holly starts in the lead then comes back to the crowd. She removes her blindfold and those of the other two women amid a chorus of carefree giggles and gyrations. Chris peels the men's blindfolds off and weaves through the crowd.

"Right this way to tonight's second act of 'carnal knowledge.'" A few twists and turns later the detective leads the group to the evening's last stop. All in their party look around in amazement, Chris watching as every set of eyes fills with desire. The last of the chaperones backs out of the room, locking it behind him. "I told you you'd all like it, didn't I?" then pausing for effect. "And the best is yet to come," Ravello says. The group follows him on a tour of the expansive room, the ladies running their hands over the shiny stirrups of the exam tables that double as kinky sex stations. They share a knowing look and lustful leer as the men watch, dumbfounded.

"Here, Kim, let me help you settle in. That particular model maximizes penetration angle, both forward and rearward," the detective says with a smile as he helps Kim, then the other woman, into position. Holly does the same with the men. Steve takes his place in iron shackles suspended from the faux dungeon wall. Anthony, the taller of the two, ambles onto a rack and smiles at Holly as she secures him in place.

Kim is the first to suspect something is amiss. Her beautiful Asian face contorts, then assumes a look of doe-eyed innocence. "How are we gonna have fun all spread out like this?"

A well-concealed electric door slides open with a hiss.

In steps Durand and one of his men, Durand dressed from head to toe in black. "Good evening, friends, thank you for coming. You are among the lucky few who will lead mankind toward the New Order. Our festivities will now kick into high gear. Sit back and relax—if you can."

Durand turning, faces Detective Ravello, giving him an icy stare. "Glove up, Doctor. We have specimens to process."

Michelle stares at the monitors, her earlier apathy gone, horrified by what is unfolding. She gasps as the words slip softly from her lips, "Oh God, Chris, no."

Chris does as he's told, donning the skull cap, mask, gown, and gloves provided for him. Durand does the same. It's been a year since he's worn scrubs, but despite the bizarre circumstances, Ravello feels strangely at home and at peace with myself.

Perplexed, Holly yells, "What the hell—?" as Durand's man restrains and gags her, dragging her through the electric door.

"Let's begin with this one," Durand say as he strokes the man's upper arm, "Tony, I believe, is it not?"

Their victim struggles to break free, biceps, shoulders, and torso straining against his restraints. Durand plunges a syringe into his jugular and delivers the paralytic medication succinylcholine.

Kim looks on in horror as Tony goes limp. "Tony! Baby!"

Durand ignores Kim's pleas and those of the other two captives.

"Please do join me, Detective. The right side of the table is all yours. I'll take this side," Durand says as he settles in on the left. Two men come through the door. The surgical assistant wheels two Mayo stands into place filled with instruments as the other man, dressed in scrubs, slides a cart adorned with masks, syringes, and inhalational anesthetics to the head of the bed. The man moves quickly, first to secure a tube down Tony's throat and then to administer general anesthetics.

Kim and the others scream all the louder as they struggle to free themselves from the same fate.

Ravello hones in on Durand as he settles into place. "It's been quite a while. I'm sure I'm rusty." Creases form at the edge of his mask, hinting at the hideous smile that lurks beneath.

"Quite all right, Detective. I shall be your guide. Continue to trust in me and I assure you, we shall be unstoppable."

Ravello has no other choice. Comply or never see Michelle again.

The detective has always tried to bend life to his will, with the same result, heartache, pain, and death for those he loves. He can't handle being a failure anymore. There has to be a better way, one that frees him of the pressure of always being in control, one that ends all their suffering and leads to rebirth.

Durand and the surgical assistant finish prepping and draping Tony, dabbing excess Betadine from his skin. Chris isn't sure why they take all of the normal surgical precautions; this patient isn't expected to outlive his surgery. "Let's take a liver and pancreas from this one, Detective."

Chris's eyes met Durand's, whose are cold, hard, and empty. Durand flicks his head from the assistant toward Ravello. A glistening blue, number twelve, titanium scalpel appears before the former surgeon turned detective. He stands rigid and still. "A midline incision to start with, Doctor," Durand instructs, a suction catheter posed in his gloved hands. Chris stares at the freshly shaven abdomen, hovering just above it with his scalpel.

"Doctor..."

His hand wavers for a few seconds before he finalizes his decision. Ravello's blade pierces skin.

Michelle's voice cries out in anguish as her hands ball up into fists, "Nooo!"

Chris's blade glides through subcutaneous tissue, Durand drinking up the blood with his catheter, cauterizing as he goes along.

There's no turning back now.

Below the subcutaneous tissue is the abdominal cavity, home to the precious organs Durand is so intent on harvesting. Durand's suctioning skills are piss poor—Ravello's hands are drenched in blood as Durand coaxes him on. A tiny ember awakens in Chris as he enjoys performing surgery again after so long. Durand is oblivious to it all.

"Excellent, Detective. Your skills seem quite intact," Durand murmurs. "Now for—"

"Boss, we've got a problem!"

Durand and Ravello lock eyes on Gerry Buehler as he storms into the room. Hours earlier Chris learned of the pharmacist's involvement with Durand's work. Kennedy and Ravello had gotten at least some things right about the investigation.

"What is it?" Durand demands.

"The cops have us surrounded."

"What?" Durand says, incredulous as he looks from Gerry to Chris. Ravello rips off his gloves, flinging them on the surgical drapes that cover the rest of Tony's body.

"I'll take care of this," Ravello says. "Grab a couple of guns and ammo, Gerry, and meet me upstairs, quickly."

Durand, regaining his composure, nods his approval.

"Go ahead. I'll send the guards after them and then assist you upstairs. Hurry!"

With that, Gerry and Chris race off to the fight of their lives.

MICHELLE'S CAPTIVITY 3

DESPAIR

▷ Chapter 1 ◁

Michelle lifts her head out of her hands. Police? Her salty tears dry as fierce determination fills her face. Rick and she stand tall, sizing each other up, poised for what is to come.

Tony, frozen in place, looks at the monitor dumbfounded. What now?

The answer comes quickly as his cell phone rings. "Hello?"

Durand's voice snarls at him. "Grab the girl and the bag and put the plan in effect. I'll catch up with you later."

Tony stares at his phone a moment, still in shock as Michelle charges forward. Her right foot hurtles through the air on a collision course with the soft cartilage of Rick's windpipe.

§

Michelle's clone, controlled by the nanometer sized devices that course through her, acts, thinks, and feels like the real Michelle. She stares at the TV monitors, her mouth agape as she tries to process what is happening. The call from Durand comes in. "Everyone get out here on the double and kill the intruders, now!" Guards grab guns off the rack behind "Michelle" and spring past her on each side, the last one locking the door from the outside as he exits.

The scene unfolds on the monitors before her. The police and FBI have the place surrounded. They'll be inside in no time, she hopes.

"Durand! You're surrounded, give it up!" King's amplified voice booms through the ground floor rooms.

§

Rick throws his hands up, absorbing the brunt of Michelle's kick as she topples him backward, her bound hands slamming his head back onto the floor as she lands on top of him. She moves quickly, interlacing her fingers and swinging her hands above her head. A crunching sound rings out from Rick's nose as Michelle's fists crash into his face. Blood spurts across it. Rick throws his hands and arms into the posture of a battered fighter as Michelle's hands slam into him again and again.

Tony's eyes dart toward the bag across the room—

too far away. Reaching for his gun, he charges toward her, taking aim as he's almost on top of her.

§

"We're not coming out without a fight, RJ," yells Chris as he peels off two shots. The bullets ricochet off the police cars in front of King.

"What the—? Have you gone loco, Ravello? We're on the same side, boy, remember?"

"Not anymore, RJ. I'm not wasting my time with the NYPD or the Bureau anymore. You guys are the reason Michelle was kidnapped and killed. You never let me go after Durand the right way after the attack on her. I could have nailed him before this all spiraled out of control," the detective yells as he rips off another shot in King's direction.

§

Caught up in the adrenaline rush and tunnel vision of combat, Michelle doesn't see Tony until he's a step away, gun drawn, aimed at her skull. In the midst of pummeling Rick, her arms swing down toward his face, then change course, using his chest as a gymnastics horse. She folds her chest, neck, and head forward, lifting and pivoting her legs, sending them flying into a surprised Tony's outstretched hand. The gun flies across the room, sliding on the smooth hardwood floor and under a large, brown ottoman.

Michelle's momentum lands her awkwardly on the floor in between her assailants. Rick, blood covering his face, gathers himself and slowly rises. Tony, enraged about the gun, pounces on her, his large frame pinning her back to the ground, driving the air out of her lungs as Michelle flops about, trying to break free.

Michelle stares at the scene unfolding on the monitor as she struggles under Tony's weight. *So hard to breathe.*

Tony grabs her arms and pins them over her head, then straddles her legs with his. Her eyes lock in on the battle Chris is waging elsewhere in the com-pound as she tries to get loose:

"Chris! It's me," Kennedy bellows. "You can't do this. I know you're out of your mind with grief over Michelle, but this isn't the answer. You're gonna get yourself killed…. Think about the kids. What are Christine and James gonna do without you?"

"Traitor! I figured out it's been you all along, Kev. You're Durand's cop on the inside! No wonder he's been able to keep a couple of steps ahead of us. None of this would have happened without you."

"Chris, you're not thinking straight. Come on out so we can talk this over. How could I be in with Durand," Kennedy says as he steps forward from behind the squad car. His hands are raised near his chest. He's completely vulnerable. "How do you explain Durand almost killing me if we're in cahoots?" Kennedy pleads.

Ravello's 9 mm semiautomatic answers for him. He lights into Kennedy, two shots ripping through his chest. Blood splatters everywhere. Kennedy flies back over the car. Hands lunge at him, pulling him behind cover.

Tony leers down at Michelle, oblivious to the action on the monitor. Michelle's eyes are wide with disbelief, her mouth agape as Tony leans his face forward and taunts her. "Got you right where I want you, toots."

§

Chris jumps back from the window, then ducks down low as bullets riddle the wall behind him. Durand stumbles alongside him, out of breath. The spray of bullets stops.

Arms and legs immobilized by Tony, brain starved of oxygen, Michelle slams her head into Tony's. The concussive blow knocks the degenerate back as Michelle wiggles free, delivering a solid kick to his head that sends him reeling. Michelle smiles with delight, unaware Rick looms right behind her.

§

"Impressive, Doctor Ravello. But let's grab your

wife and get the hell out of here while we can. We'll take the tunnel and live to fight another day." Durand leaps up, then runs full tilt. Chris races behind him, through the labyrinth's many twists and turns, wondering where the hell they are.

Footsteps come crashing toward them—closer, closer.

Durand flicks a few wall switches along the way. Walls shift, barriers appearing from nowhere. *What the hell? This is not to be believed!* Navigating this place by himself would have been impossible for Ravello.

"We're almost to your beloved. A few steps more and we're home free." Despite the barriers the footsteps pound just behind them now.

"Is it really Michelle or just another Durand sleight of hand? I've got to know before I see her."

Durand pauses and looks at the detective—with concern and empathy. The floor is trembling under the barrage heading toward them. "I too have known loss, Chris. Far more than you could ever imagine. My work will bring a new, better order to life on planet earth. It is what I live for. But that will have to wait. Right now I present to you your dearly beloved."

Durand springs them through a door as the wall behind them comes crashing down. Chris's wife's clone is recoiled at the far end of the room, arms behind her back, eyes locked on a monitor above her.

"Michelle!" he races toward her.

§

Michelle's eyes dart to the monitor, catching Chris as he's reunited with the clone. Thick arms encircle her, lifting her from the ground. Her legs flail about. "What the hell?" she says as Tony shakes his head and gets up from the floor.

Rick: "Grab her legs, Tone."

He eyes the bag as a smile emerges. "I've got a better idea."

§

"You killed your best friend in cold blood, and you're helping this madman carve up innocent people? Chris, how could you?" Tears stream down the clone's crimson face. Her words stop Chris in his tracks. "Michelle" stares at Durand now. The detective has never seen that look of pure anger and hatred before on her face. A gun appears from behind her back as she screams at Durand. "You made him do these things to save me! You bastard!"

The FBI is bearing down on them. The door flies open behind Chris as he yells, "Michelle, put the gun down. Don't shoot!"

§

Tony rifles through the bag as Michelle's legs kick wildly at the air.

Rick grimaces as Michelle's right foot strikes his kneecap, but he holds her tight. "For God's sake, Tone, hurry the fuck up."

Tony throws open a small case in the bag that holds a single, labeled syringe. Oughtta do the trick.

Michelle's teeth sink into Rick's left shoulder, "Aaarrgh!" But he holds her like a vise. She shakes from side to side as Tony approaches her with the uncapped syringe, a few drops dripping from its needle.

$

Shots ring out. The smell of gunpowder fills the air as Chris slips to the ground and tries crawling forward on the floor. Blood pools in front of him.

Feds and the NYPD blow past him on each side. They grab Durand first. Then one takes hold of him.

"I'm so sorry, Chris. There was no other way," the agent says, sadness washed across his face. "She would have killed you."

Michelle is heaped in front of Chris, blood billowing out of her, filling the floor between them.

"No! She had the gun pointed at Durand, not me, you idiot!"

$

Tony grabs Michelle's face and roughly thrusts it away as he plunges the needle into her neck. Her eyes grow wide with horror as Tony empties the drug into her, a burning sensation tearing through her neck as the drug enters her bloodstream. She screams and throws herself violently about, trying to break free before the drug's effects take hold. Her eyelids grow heavy as energy drains from her body. Her movements slow to a standstill as hope of an escape is extinguished. One last glimpse of Chris fills her mind before she slips away:

Chris lunges forward, hysterical, out of his mind. He pulls the woman he believes is Michelle toward him, cradling her head in his lap. Her eyes and face are sallow, lifeless. "No! No! Not my Michelle! Not again...."

▷ Chapter 2 ◁

Tony dumps Michelle's limp body onto the twin bed, handcuffing her right wrist to the bedpost. "Lot fucking heavier than she looks."

Rick looks on, wincing as his hand runs along the bandages on his swollen nose. "So, what do we do now?" he asks as he dumps Michelle's bags on the floor and stares at her, angry over the beating she gave him.

Tony wipes his forehead with the back of his hand as he heads out of the bedroom. Exhaling, he says, "Figure out what the fuck happened to the boss." He surveys the small kitchen, noticing mold and mildew stains throughout the grout and numerous old stains from coffee mugs. Shaking his head, he trudges into the small living room/dining room, plops down on a cheap, black leather sofa, and flicks on the TV. An attractive, blonde newscaster reports the latest. "In a stunning early morning raid in the sleepy bedroom community of Briarcliff Manor, The NYPD and FBI have captured the crazed serial killer, Dr. Jean Louis Durand." A picture of Durand from better days stands next to the anchor's face. "Details remain sketchy, but at least one fatality is confirmed, that of Michelle Ravello, wife of NYPD Division Chief and former surgeon, Dr. Christopher Ravello." Durand's picture disappears, replaced by a split screen of the news anchor and an on-scene reporter. "Any information on where Durand is now, John?"

The reporter shakes his head. "Afraid not, Meghan. NYPD has offered no official comment yet. Best guess is they are busy interrogating him or possibly have him at Rikers Island."

The blonde nods. "Thanks, John." The screen goes whole again. "In other top stories, a three alarm fire rages in the Williamsburg section of—"

Tony clicks off the TV, then mutters, "Fuckin' A."

Rick stares down, his shoe tracing an imaginary design on the floor. "So now what?"

"We keep her tucked away till Durand gets word to us."

Rick regards Tony with caution. "You heard the news; Boss is at Rikers. How the hell's he gonna get word to us?"

Tony reaches over and picks up the bag he brought over from Durand's lab, drops it in his lap, and sifts through it. Eyes on its content, he says, "Boss had all the angles covered, including what to do if he was caught." Tony stops his searching, looks at Rick. "He's got all sorts of cool shit in here, including…" jerking his head toward the bedroom that houses Michelle, "stuff to keep the bitch in line."

Rick smiles while nodding his head slowly. "Cool." He rubs his nose again. "Definitely looking for pay back after what she done to me. How long till someone gets word to us?"

Tony offers a weary grunt. "Week, maybe two."

Rick's eyes roll skyward. "What? Why so long?"

Tony tosses the bag aside and rises to his full height. He grabs Rick by the shirt, spitting the words out, "Heats all over Durand right now. No way he makes a move till things cool off. 'Sides, our mole at the NYPD, he'll need time to get word back and forth from the boss."

Rick leans his face away from Tony and nods with deference. "So where's that leave us?"

Tony looks around the cramped two-bedroom with disdain as he lets go of the shirt. He pulls a few bills out of his wallet and stuffs them in Rick's hand. "Grab some shut eye, then go to the store and get some Ajax and other cleaning shit. This place is a fuckin' mess." He shakes his head. "And none of us are going anywhere anytime soon."

§

Michelle's eyes flutter open, her head aching and filled with cobwebs. *Where the hell?*

A sharp pain cuts through the center of her skull as she looks at her left hand, surprised the rope is gone. A tug confirms the worst about her right as handcuffs rattle against the steel bedpost. Blinking, she adjusts her eyes to the dim surroundings. A nondescript wooden side table, no frills lamp, and a beat up old wooden chair are all the furniture the room offers. To the left an open closet, her bags slumped in front of it on the floor. Straight ahead and to the right, two doors leading where?

Time to find out.

Michelle moves slowly, the pain in her head unrelenting and joined now by an aching back and chest. She eases her feet to the floor and inches forward without a sound, her free hand straining to reach the door to her right, but it's no use. Too far away. She lets out a frustrated sigh and turns back toward the bed, looking for anything else of interest. Anything that offers a clue about where the hell she is.

Blinds drawn all the way down, she hears the din of traffic and commotion coming from the street below. She slides past the bed, the cuff cutting into her right wrist as she strains to reach the window sill. *Come on, just a little bit more.*

Her fingertips quiver as the blinds remain just out of reach. She leans all her weight toward the window, pulling the cuff chain taut, but the bed remains fixed in place as the cuff cuts deeper into her skin.

Fuck! What now?

She slumps back toward the bed, her tired brain unable to conjure up alternate plans. Taking a deep breath, she collapses onto the bed, disheartened and drained by the day's events. An hour passes, sleep eluding her as her mind obsessively replays the battle with Tony and Rick, Chris's bizarre behavior during the police siege, and her crushing defeat as she tried to escape.

A fitful sleep finally befalls her, Michelle thrashing in the bed as her nightmares continue their reign over her.

▷ Chapter 3 ◁

Gate of Heaven Cemetery

Gagged and bound, a tearful and despondent Michelle stares down the long hill at the bizarre, yet familiar scene: her burial. The crowd is much smaller this time. No kids, friends, deacon, or coworkers. Michelle strains to see through her tears as the cold wind stings her face. She longs to be with her husband, to wipe away his pain by showing him the woman he is burying now after the FBI shooting is not his dear wife, but just another impostor created by Durand. A sad smile forms on Michelle's face as Chris comes into focus. Bundled in a long, gray, wool coat, he stands to the left of two cemetery workers busy digging up the grave where the first clone of her is buried and where Chris will lay to rest Michelle's second clone.

On Chris's left a towering figure, donning his own coat, his back turned toward her. Michelle blinks and squints her eyes, trying in vain to clear her view. At six feet three inches not many men tower over her husband, so who could it be?

The hulk turns toward Chris, his profile confusing her. *Kevin Kennedy still alive?* She saw him pummeled by bullets from Chris's gun, blood shooting everywhere the day of her failed escape. Her spirit is buoyed as warmth diffuses through Michelle's heart. Maybe there's hope for her too. She looks to her left and right at Tony and Rick for any glimmer of reaction or recognition then laughs inwardly. As if these idiots could hold any answers.

The workers lift the coffin out of the grave, stumbling as they set it on the ground. One man brushes dirt off its surface while the other man points excitedly at it and simulates a lifting motion. Chris, looking perplexed, waves both men off and crouches between the two clone's coffins. Michelle blinks rapidly, her heart a twisted mess as Chris glances at one of the workers, then lifts the coffin's cover. Her eyes go wide. These last few weeks have been terrifying and insane, but nothing prepared her for this.

Rick and Tony smile with deep satisfaction as a stunned Chris Ravello falls back from the empty coffin, his head vacillating between it and the dead clone. Michelle's head darts between her captors as she strains to speak, her eyes imploring them to release the gag. Tony grabs her cheeks between his meaty fingers and winks at Michelle. "Surprise, surprise, toots. Bet you'd love to know what the hell's going on with that first clone of you?" He chuckles, holding in a heartier laugh for fear it would alert Ravello and Kennedy to their presence.

§

Kennedy rushes over to his friend, pulling up as he looks in the coffin. "What the fuck?"

Ravello and he lock eyes, Kennedy speaking first. "I don't get it. Where the hell's the body we already buried?"

Chris shakes his head, trying to make sense of it. "No idea." Hands wrapped around his folded knees, Ravello rocks back and forth as he mulls over the possibilities. The two workers stand in stunned silence as seconds drag by before a shaken Ravello reengages his friend. "There weren't any more clones, Michelle or otherwise, when the team canvassed Durand's place, right?"

Kennedy takes a knee beside his friend. "Right and kinda weird. All that high-tech equipment and no new bodies in the pipeline."

Chris shakes his head, recalling the details of the investigation. "Just doesn't add up. And we never found most of the info on his experiments either."

"Think he moved stuff to another lab, had a back-up somewhere?" Kennedy asks weakly.

Chris shakes his head again. "Doubt it. Lab like that must cost millions and take years to put together. Don't see how he could have another one."

Kennedy and Ravello stare straight ahead, their eyes boring a hole in the empty coffin before Kennedy rises up and helps his friend do the same. Jutting his head toward the body, "So, what do you figure? One was the clone, one was Michelle?"

Ravello stares at the body, a blank look on his face. Slowly wringing his hands, "My money's on the missing body being the clone and this being Michelle." Ravello drops down beside the corpse. "I spoke with her. Seemed like Michelle.... Don't think he could've pulled that off with just a clone."

"What if there was only one body all along?" Kennedy's voice offers a faint hope. "He digs it up, re-activates it somehow? Or he had two clones of Michelle, both dead, and she's alive?"

Ravello smiles weakly. "Pretty doubtful, my friend, but thanks for trying." Chris fights back tears as he bows his head, but one breaks free, falling on the dead woman's body as he mumbles, "Goodbye baby."

❯ Chapter 4 ❮

Back at the safe house, Michelle is stuck in an all too familiar position—chained to her bed. She stares at the ceiling while Tony and Rick banter and holler, amusing themselves with yet another stupid game. She glares at her bags on the floor. Untouched and out of her reach, they're the last vestiges of her life back home, and her best hope at getting the hell out of here. She's weary, homesick, and angry. Four weeks chained to this damn bed. Four weeks missing her babies and Chris so much it's tearing her insides apart. Four weeks of deepening despair and mounting anxiety, a screaming voice imploring her to escape—RIGHT NOW!

But she can't.

She'll only get one shot at it, and the right combination of timing and circumstances still eludes her.

A tear runs down Michelle's tired face as she tamps down on her feelings, chides herself to be patient just a little longer.

Tony lays down his cards with a smile, "Gin," then paws at his winnings, pulling the crinkled bills toward himself. Rick slams down his cards. "Didn't know any better, I'd think you was cheating. Nobody's this frigging lucky." Tony taps the side of his head. "Brains, not luck." Then with a smug expression he says, "That's why you ain't won one."

Rick collects the cards, tossing them to the side as he strums his fingers on the table. "Whatever." Tony breaks the seal on a new bottle and pours himself a drink of whiskey. Rick looks at him with contempt, "Sure you should be doing that again?"

Tony glares back at him.

"Can't afford to get sloshed with you-know-who in the next room."

"It's one fucking drink, moron. What're you, my old lady?" he grumbles, holding the glass in the direction of Michelle's bedroom. "'Sides, bitch is cuffed to the bed. She ain't going nowhere."

Michelle grits her teeth as her eyes bore a hole through tweedle dee's skull. Drink up, you fat bastard. You've got no idea what's in store for you.

◊ Chapter 5 ◊

Weeks of planning, of waiting for the heat to die down, of figuring which palms to grease and when. The police officer forces his way forward, flashes his badge at two underage drinkers, scattering them from their corner seats at the crowded bar and claiming them for his own.

"What're you having?" the burly, scruff-faced bartender asks in a gruff voice.

"Killian's Red for me and my friend."

The bartender glances at the empty seat, then pulls on the draft handle.

The exchange of funds and fluids complete, the officer glances at his watch, takes a long drag on his drink. A few minutes pass before a chunky, aged brunette circles in like a vulture, her bright red dress and glowing makeup screaming "prostitute." She saunters up, puts a hand on his shoulder, and shows him her nicotine stained enamels. "Need a date, handsome?"

Looking straight ahead, he says, "Beat it, before I bust you."

The hooker's smile dims. "Least it'd be less crowded in the slammer," then she melts into the sea of bodies.

Ten more minutes come and go before the off-duty corrections officer shows up, the mole barking at him, "You're late."

The CO, blonde hair trimmed close to his scalp, sits in front of his waiting beer and drains half of the glass. "Place is fucking packed. Better chance of spotting you at The Meadowlands."

The officer looks straight ahead, a thin smile parting his small face as he waves off the approaching bartender.

"Got it?"

Crew cut reaches for his inside jacket pocket but the mole's words halt him. "Not yet. Milk the rest of your drink."

The corrections officer looks around casually then complies as the mole teases a small wad of bills from his coat and surreptitiously hands them under the counter. The guard glances at the wad, grabs it, and imbibes twice more before his moneyed hand disappears into his jacket pocket. It re-emerges under the bar with the envelope. The mole pockets it and makes small talk for the next two minutes before rising and tossing a few twenties on the counter. "Dinner's on me. Knock yourself out." Then he disappears into the throng.

$

Rat-a-tat-tat. Rat-a-tat-tat.

Tony draws his gun as he approaches the peep hole in the front door and looks through. A smile emerges as the gun disappears. 'Bout time. He nods toward Rick, who marches over and locks Michelle in her room.

Tony opens the door, shepherding in the mole. The men exchange a quick shake, Tony patting him on the back as they lean toward each other. "Been a bitch getting through to him?" Tony asks.

The man nods, his eyes darting around the small apartment he selected and secured for such situations. "Hell yeah. Gotta lay low for a while after this." His eyes fix on Tony. "Got any Jack?"

"Always." Tony throws two glasses down, pouring them shots as they settle in. "So, what's the word?"

The mole smiles broadly as he pulls the letter from his pocket. "He's figured a way out."

"No shit?" Tony's voice fills with surprise.

The NYPD mole puts the letter on the table, slides it over. "All in here." The smile turns dark and sinister. "And best of all it involves torturing the bitch."

$

Michelle slips the bobby pin back into her hair and carefully lowers the open cuff to the bed post. Nobody will be in now to check on her. They're too preoccupied with their secret plans. Without a sound she slides along the floor and presses her head against the door, straining to make the words out.

"...involves torturing the bitch."

"Like the sound of that."

Guttural laughter fills the room. Michelle's brow furrows. Minutes of dead silence. *What the hell?*

Chairs sliding across the floor, a stampede of lumbering footsteps. The front door slamming shut?

Shit!

Michelle bolts to the bed, secures the handcuff to her right wrist, and assumes a look of boredom atop the bed.

She peers at the door, waiting, her gut bound in knots. Footfalls grow louder then cease. A key clanks in the lock, the door handle turning...

▷ Chapter 6 ◁

Ravello emerges from the NYPD psychiatrist's office, dropping to a knee in the anteroom as he gives Christine and James a big hug. His dad's eyes search his. "How'd it go?"

Chris draws a deep breath. A forceful exhale as he rises to his full height. "As well as can be expected."

Bill and Chris shepherd the kids to the car, riding in silence back to Westchester, Chris's brain a swirl of disconnected, competing thoughts, his heart heavy, trampled with unfathomable loss. Thirty, in the prime of her life. Two beautiful young children. A loving marriage. How is it possible she's really gone?

Guilt claws at his throat. He wishes it would close in on him, finish him off. His decision to leave a life of comfort and riches behind, to walk away from the career he and his wife worked tirelessly to build. All so he could hunt down the depraved in the wake of his mother's attack.

A tear rolls down his left cheek. Didn't count on the depraved striking back, killing the love of his life, robbing his children of the light of theirs, leaving their father a shell of a man.

Chris steers the car north on the NYS Thruway, his dad staring out the window as the miles roll by, his children fast asleep. An unexpected and slight smile emerges from the grief as he looks in the rearview at little James. At Christine, her fifth birthday just a few weeks away. So innocent and beautiful. They deserve so much better.

Anger flares up in him then melts away. He resolves to make it so. He'll let the upcoming Thanksgiving holiday come and go quietly, but right after he'll take care of it.

Big changes ahead for him and his family.

§

Rick storms into the room and pounces on Michelle as Tony makes his preparations a room away. She lashes out with her left hand and knee, Rick deflecting the blows. "Not this time, bitch. This time your ass is mine." He twists her face down on the bed, releases the cuffs from the post, secures both hands behind her back. Yanking her up by her hair, he pushes her forward. She stumbles, falls to the ground, bloodying her lips. Rick smiles and hoists her up, drives her onward.

Michelle's eyes go wide as she sees what's laid out for her.

"Get her back on the table so we can tie her down," Tony grumbles.

Rick moves with confidence and skill, forcing Michelle down amid her screams and struggles. She's uncuffed and recuffed again. Her arms and legs hang down over the edges of the table, cuffed wrists tied to her ankles and pulled taut. She shrieks again, then spits the words out.

"What the hell are you doing?"

Tony brandishes the instrument. Michelle blinks twice. She's seen it before, but where, when?

Shit, the injector... from Area Four of Durand's lab. Oh God, no.

"Boss's got big plans for you, toots." Tony holds the sharp tip of the instrument in front of her eyes. "You're his ticket out of Rikers—imagine that." He moves his chin side to side. In a condescending, patronizing tone he says, "Can't take a chance, though." He leans his face toward hers, his whiskey breath assaulting her. A sick smile. "Gotta make sure you do exactly what we want ya to."

Michelle snaps her head toward Tony, feigning a head butt. He pulls back as she smiles. "What makes you think that damn thing will work on me? Durand's only used it on clones."

Tony grabs the letter in his hand, shakes it at her. "Boss seems to think it'll work. Guess we're gonna find out real soon." Tony laughs as he stares intently at Michelle. "This'll either get you in line or..."

"Or what?" she screams.

Tony eyes his partner, a sadistic smile forming. "Hubby thinks she's dead already. No big deal if it don't work out." Tony bares his teeth. "Now hold her down."

§

Durand mills about the barren yard at the Otis Bantum Correctional Facility, one of four such pits of depravity at Rikers that house adult male offenders. Baby killers, deviants who torture and kill pregnant women, are welcome prey for their fellow lecherous inmates.

But not so with Durand.

News of the sociopath doctor's gruesome experiments in human cloning tore through the prison population like a pestilence, sowing fear over what the Frankensteinian physician is capable of.

Even the most hardened, debased criminals steer clear of Durand or offer him their unflagging allegiance.

The wind swirls and fluctuates, kicking dirt and dust into Durand's eyes as he stares off the island at the chilled waters of the East River. He blinks his soulless eyes, scattering the debris as his mind replays the events of July 4th. A shoot out, Ravello chasing him down, a seeming victory for him over Durand.

Until she appeared and changed everything. Offered him a way out. A way to torture dear Detective Ravello in the most unexpected and delightful manner. A narrow smile breaks through.

Time to make use of her all over again.

§

Michelle grapples and screams, her voice dying out as the injector's needle rips through the scar in her neck. Tony's face hardens as he pulls the trigger, emptying the vial's entire contents into her jugular vein. Searing pain as the hot fluid, with its nanometer sized cargo, penetrates her bloodstream, aiming to destroy her volition.

The bitch's wailing stops. Her eyes bulge as if ready to break free, then fall back, becoming vacant as her face slackens. Boss said it would only take a minute to kick in, then they'd know.

Tony glances at Rick, nervous with the excitement of uncertainty. Turns his eyes back toward her. A wave of tension rolls through her body. Her eyes become still, catatonic.

Tony and Rick's eyes meet again, their confidence cresting. A sneer emerges on Rick's face, his eyes filling with lust. "Can do whatever the hell we want to her now."

His comrade waves a hand in front of Michelle's eyes. No reaction. A sick smile on his face as he straddles her, leaning in, his hot, rank breath heavy on her again.

Saliva sprays from her lips, covering his face as she jerks and twists her body. Shock and pain as he teeters, then falls from the table, crashing to the floor. A victorious smile engulfs her, her eyes shining with defiance. "Better luck next time, loser."

▷ Chapter 7 ◁

Monday, November 30th, One Police Plaza.

Ravello chats with Commissioner of Police, John Kelly's secretary, Diana D. His insides twisted in knots, he nonetheless puts on a lighthearted and carefree appearance.

"...I'll probably go back up to the Vineyard for a while. My buddy's got a lobster boat up there and remodels homes in the off-season. Dad said he'd come up with me and help me take care of the kids while I sort a few things out. The hard work and isolation will do me some good. I've heard the Vineyard is—"

Diana picks up the phone on the first ring. "Commissioner Kelly will see you now, Detective Ravello," she says in her most official manner before softening with a warm smile. "And good luck with everything, Chris."

He's through the door and shaking Kelly's hand in no time, a weird, out of body feeling rippling through Ravello.

"Been a rough few months, Detective. What can I do for you?" Kelly says as he motions him toward a seat in front of the Commissioner's large maple desk.

"I'll stand, Sir. This won't take long."

"Suit yourself," he says with a puzzled, hard look as he sits down.

Chris steadies himself on the edge of the desk and begins.

"It's been an insane year, Sir, chasing down criminals. The ghosts of my mother and her killers have always been close by, the wind at my back, pushing me—always onward and upward. But this Durand case, it's taken more than its toll on me, Sir." He pulls his badge, ID, and gun out of his pocket and slides them across the desk to Kelly, who glances at them before locking in on Ravello's eyes.

"We all go through it, Chris. It's part of the job," Kelly says, a hint of his Brooklyn accent breaking through. He slides the gun, ID, and badge back toward his Division Chief as he continues, "And at the end of your career with the NYPD, all the insanity fades to black and you're left a better man for having served the greatest city in the world." Kelly rises to just short of Ravello's height. "Take a few more weeks off, enjoy some time with the kids. We'll see you back just after the New Year," Kelly says as he rests a hand on Chris's shoulder and smiles.

"Afraid I can't do that, Sir." Chris averts his eyes, choking back the emotion. "A lot has changed since I joined the NYPD. I'm a widower now with two beautiful young children. I was just about at peace with my mother's death when Michelle was taken from me. Should have never happened," he says with a shake of his head as he fights back tears. "If it wasn't for what I said to Kev during our theatrics, she wouldn't have been confused, wouldn't have lashed out at me... wouldn't have been killed." The detective's voice trails off as he bows his head, a few tears running down the sides of his face. The pain is searing, too much to handle. He bends forward a bit, resists clutching his chest. He can't allow himself to have an attack here. One reason for leaving now is to avoid them finding out about his disease, about falsifying his medical records.

"Chris, are you okay?" Kelly says as his eyes seek out Ravello's.

In another moment he'll have no way to support his family, but he'll have honor and the respect of his family and friends, and those he has worked with in law enforcement. That will vanish if they learn he's a fraud, a liar.

He needs to wrap this up quickly.

Straightening up, through gritted teeth he presses on. "Too much time spent chasing demons. I need to know if there is a better way for me. Thank you for everything, Sir." He walks around to get closer to Kelly. Patting him on the shoulder, he shakes his hand, then turns and walks out the door.

As he heads out of One Police Plaza, Ravello is a whirlwind of thoughts and emotions.

He was really good at being a cop. He had a lot to offer, and the work made him feel good. But he also has a body that's breaking down, betraying him with attacks that are more frequent and severe. Doctors warned him: unchecked, the pheo would lead to severe and crippling organ damage, disability, and death. Christine and James have lost one parent. He can't let them lose another.

Walking away from the NYPD, Chris feels like a failure once again. How will he support his family? How will he fulfill his vow to his mother to make the world a better place in her name? Would he ever hold down a meaningful job again?

He climbs into the Firebird and starts the engine.

A year ago he failed at medicine.

Now he had to walk away from police work that used his medical training.

He shifts the car into gear and eases out of the parking space.

Ravello isn't sure what he'll do with himself now, but he'll figure it out, he knows he will... for Michelle, for the kids... for Ma... and for himself.

§

"...that's all I know."

A grim Durand nods to the guard as the guard distances himself from the cell. Durand says in a soft voice, "Not what I wanted to hear, but thank you."

The Giver lashes out at his bed, kicking the mattress again and again before throwing it on the floor. The metal bunk bed frame wobbles as his roommate calls out, "Watch what the hell you're—" his voice dying in his throat as his eyes meet Durand's withering glare.

The killer skulks about his cage, rage boiling over as he mumbles to himself, replaying the conversation. *Failed to control her? How the hell is that even possible? Just inject the bitch and watch her fall under your spell.*

He shakes his head as he paces in a tight arc, his roommate casting him a perplexed look.

"What the hell's your problem?"

The roomie averts his eyes, burying his head in his book as he rereads the same paragraph for the fourth time.

Durand grinds his teeth as his steps slow. He leans against the wall, straddling the tiny barred window. *Resigning? What the hell for? You finally nailed me, you idiot!*

He'll need them both to pull off his plan, to get out of this wretched place. His eyes dart about, taking in the yard where the inmates recess, the barbed wire atop the fences, the guard towers beyond. His eyes study the water off in the distance. *What in God's name is that?*

Squinting, he focuses in on the rowboat, its outboard motor churning through the water as it makes the short journey from shore to the nearby island. *Can't be more than half a mile from here and much less from the island to the shore.*

Pulling into the dock, the passenger ties up the boat, then moves hurriedly toward an old building straight ahead. Crossing a short stretch of beach the figure disappears into overgrowth. Seconds later he re-emerges into a small field before entering the rickety old building. *What the hell is in there?*

The Giver's pulse slows, his breathing deepens, as his mind considers a new path to freedom.

▷ Chapter 8 ◁

It's now or never.

Six weeks stuck in this cramped, disgusting two-bedroom apartment with these losers, alternating between chained to the bed, cooking, and cleaning for the slobs.

But at least that servitude gave her the access she needed.

Tony's a room away, sucking down his midafternoon whiskey. Rick's busy with the last crime thriller from recently departed author Sue Grafton.

Michelle teases a bobby pin from deep in her hair and sticks the end of it in the cuff around her wrist. Hours of practice these past weeks make her movements deft and precise. The cuff pops open. She lowers it quietly to the bedpost and tiptoes to the bathroom.

Michelle grabs the bleach from under the sink and

the cup sitting on the edge of the sink. Unlike her days as a chem major at Fordham, there are no exacting measuring devices handy. But she won't need any.

She taps the cleaning container, the white powder spilling into the cup. Michelle grabs the ammonia and rubbing alcohol from her bags that she took from her house nearly two months ago. She lines them up on the counter. Next comes the unused cleaning rag.

Michelle pours generous amounts of rubbing alcohol and bleach on the cloth and rubs the ends together, taking care not to inhale any of the sweet-smelling, stupor-inducing fumes. She waves a hand in front of her face. Enough to knock an elephant out cold. Turning her attention to the ammonia, she smiles.

Have they ever heard of the dangers of mixing ammonia and bleach?

They're about to find out first hand.

Michelle takes great care dispensing small amounts of ammonia into the bleach. The result? The toxic and explosive liquid called hydrazine, a key component of rocket fuel. Blast off here we come!

Michelle brings the rag and cup over to the bed, resting them on the nightstand. She puts the cuff on loosely, so it appears as if in place. Now for her Academy-Award-winning performance.

She begins to moan—loudly. A minute passes with nothing to show for it.

Then footsteps. Light, likely Rick's.

The door flies open, bounces off the wall and half closes as he walks in. "What the hell's going on?"

In between gasps of pain, Michelle gets the words out, "Need to get to the bathroom quickly."

Rick does a once over on her. "What for?"

"Cramps... gonna have the runs."

A look of disgust fills his face as he walks over to free her wrist. Michelle writhes in pain until the moment he reaches for the cuff. In a whirl she grabs the cloth in her right hand, sandwiching his mouth, nose, and face with her palms. Rick's eyes go wide, his body limp before he can mount a countermove. Michelle catches him, straining with all her might as she lowers him to the floor and listens.

Nothing.

She takes the cup in one hand and moves with stealth, crawling on the floor to the door. Now on her knees, she moves toward the couch, the back of Tony's fat head just two feet in front of her. Michelle coils her body, ready to lunge forward and throw the caustic material in his face.

Her sock slips on the hardwood floor instead!

She comes crashing down, the cup breaking, material spilling everywhere. Tiny bubbles burn on the floor like lava. Tony spins around, gun pointed at her face in a millisecond. Michelle's head slumps to the floor, her heart broken that she'll miss her little girl's big birthday tomorrow.

Tony hustles around the couch and grabs her arm. "Looks like you'll be staying just a little longer, toots."

▷ Chapter 9 ◁

Jean Louis Durand clicks rapidly on the mouse, jumping between several open browsers in the prison's library. It's taken nearly six weeks of legal wrangling by his attorney to get him this access and he intends to make the most of it. His eyes skim the article from April 12, 2014.

After fierce debate, The New York City Council on Monday approved plans for Doctor Harold Hyslop and his Institute of Immunologic Breakthroughs to renovate and occupy the last remaining structure on North Brother Island, one-time home of the infamous "Typhoid Mary" back in the early 1900s. The island has a checkered past, having been the site of wreckage of the steamship the General Slocum on June 15, 1904 in which over

> *1,000 people died and in the 1950s serving as an inhumane drug treatment center, where Heroin addicts would be locked away in their rooms until the ravages of their detoxification were complete.*

Durand nods his head as he jumps between articles outlining Hyslop's "groundbreaking work in creating biologics, proteins used to elicit and control the body's immune response, to cure a wide range of diseases, including diabetes, thyroid issues, arthritis..." and some less spectacular treatment protocols, "From April to August, 2014 three patients treated for organ transplant rejection by Dr. Hyslop died. The NYPD, who investigated the deaths and ruled them accidental, and Dr. Hyslop both refused to comment for this story."

Over the next ten minutes the sociopath brushes up on Hyslop's background, noting his training at Harvard Medical School, brief childless marriage in the late 1990s, and a sappy story about how Hyslop's gravely ill brother inspired the doctor's work in treating organ transplant rejections.

Durand leans back and steeples his fingers. *How droll, pathetic, and ironic. If not for your good intentions, those three patients would still be alive.*

Mental gears engage, spinning and swiveling, as Durand mulls over the disparate facts. He has never met Hyslop before, but Durand is familiar with his earlier work. The two even shared the same source of funding for some of their research projects. Durand's head shifts side to side, his eyes sweeping the area. Nobody's paying him any mind. His fingers move in a flurry across the keyboard. Two minutes later he is hacked into Hyslop's records. Durand's eyes study the good doctor's list of current patients, when they'll receive their treatments, and who their referring doctors are.

The Giver's eyes grow large. His entire body motionless, the sociopath stares at the screen.

Ravello. Jacobs. How wonderfully fortuitous.

Durand immerses himself in the specifics of Ravello's treatment protocol. Makes mental notes on this and Jacobs. A smile emerges as he finds another interesting patient, one scheduled to have treatment in the coming weeks and whose medical history is strikingly similar to Phil Hyslop.

Durand leans back again and mulls this over, then lets out a small chuckle as the realization washes over him. *Can't wait to see how that treatment works out.*

The evil doctor spends fifteen more minutes hunched over the keyboard, learning about the inner workings of Hyslop's lab and his employees, before moving on to other topics of interest.

A quartet of other inmates mill about the small library, two restacking books and periodicals, the others searching for crime novels. A fifth reads the latest edition of The New York Times. Durand starts at the sound of an ancient landline wailing on a nearby wall. The librarian picks up the phone, nodding as she speaks. "Yes... he's right here. One moment please." She places the receiver down on her desk and signals one of the inmates, who approaches Durand, jerking a thumb at him. "Call's for you, man." Durand raises an eyebrow as he walks toward the phone.

§

Tony paces the floor. Weary and spent from the latest episode with Michelle, he's spent the last five days weighing his options. He dreads reaching out to the boss like this, but it'll be much worse for him if he stays silent and she gets away. He stares at the phone in his hand for a long time. He'd tried the mole a few times in the hope he would get word through to Durand, but he never got a call back. The man's words from their last meeting ring in his ears: "Gotta lay low for a while after this."

Tony takes a deep breath and jabs at the phone, sweat building under his arms. Ten minutes later, his shirt soaked through after getting bounced from one prison official to the next, he finally makes contact. "Gonna be real hard to keep the bitch under wraps much longer, Boss."

Durand's eyes scour his surroundings. Neither the phoneline nor this place afford privacy. *Why the hell call me like this? Can't this imbecile take care of anything?*

He chomps down on his bile and plays it coolly. "Falling behind on the rent again, is she?"

Tony stares at his phone, *What the hell...?* Then playing along, he says, "More like she's trying to break her lease."

"Well, we can't have that, now can we?" Durand replies in an exaggeratedly upbeat manner. "As landlords we need to enforce all the provisions of our arrangement, otherwise the situation devolves into anarchy."

Tony's face twists into a mess as he sighs. "Already there, Boss. Tenant's set off fireworks inside and done all sorts of shit to uh... be released from her obligations. Can I terminate the lease if need be?"

Durand's eyes narrow. "The care package I left for you, it contains some wondrous goodies, dutifully labeled. Those should help reign in our tenant's less acceptable tendencies."

Tony scratches his head, unsure what Durand is talking about. "Uh, okay... I'll give it a shot." He clears his throat. "What if it don't work, if we've still got a bull in a china shop?"

Durand's voice lowers to a whisper as he stares at the computer station he was working at. "If needed, my plan can proceed just fine with the promise of an intact tenant. Try to salvage the situation, but if it proves untenable, do whatever is necessary to extinguish the threat."

Tony's face morphs into a delighted smile as he

looks toward Michelle's room. "Thanks, Boss. I'll get right on it."

▷ Chapter 10 ◁

"**D**on't let her fucking close them," Tony shouts as he tries to jam the sedative into Michelle's mouth.

Rick pries her jaws farther apart. Exasperated, he says, "Trying... but she's pretty strong. Hurry."

Tony shoves the pill in and splashes water into her mouth. "Let her go now." Tony paws her cheeks and yells at her, "Swallow it!"

Michelle eyes him carefully, then spits the water and pill back at him. The back of his hand slams into the side of her face. "You fuckin' bitch!" Michelle's head careens off the wall, then slumps to her chest.

Tony glares at Rick. "No more mister nice guy. Hold her." Rick does as he's told while Tony batters her abdomen with blow after blow, driving the wind out of her. Michelle withers like a delicate flower starved of water. Tony halts his barrage, grabs another pill and the glass. This time she offers no resistance as he washes the sedative down her throat.

Rick slumps back, spent. He loosens his grip on Michelle as Tony stares at her. "Shouldn't be long now."

§

SMACK! Tony's hand collides with Michelle's cheek. "Not so fucking tough now, all wasted on downers." Michelle staggers and falls to the floor, dazed and disoriented. Rick grabs her from behind, copping a feel of her breasts through her blouse. He lifts her by her boobs, then twirls her around as he laughs. "Got a nice rack, baby." Michelle's eyes roll up as her head flops back.

Grabbing the sides of her face he lowers her back down as he makes the most of her impaired condition. Rubbing her face against his crotch as he makes a humping motion, he says, "Hey, while you're down there..." Rick dry humps her face a few times, then lets her crash to the ground unconscious. He picks up his drink and clinks glasses with Tony, laughing like a frat boy at an out of control party. The men laugh and drink for the next few minutes, their faces red, eyes tearing with laughter. Eventually their enthusiasm dies down and Tony speaks up. "Time to put our plaything away." Rick looks down at Michelle with derision. She looks very much like a corpse awaiting police tape. "Fucking worthless bitch." He hoists her on his shoulder and strides toward her bedroom.

As he drops her on the bed and secures the handcuff, Rick smiles, knowing he'll use his new-found control to pay her back for the beating she inflicted on him weeks earlier. He leans in and whispers to her, his breath wreaking of whiskey, "Just getting started on you."

§

Michelle's head feels like a sea-swept vessel in the midst of a raging storm as she lies on the bed. Her eyelids are like leaden weights as she strains to keep them open and focused on the action in the other room. Slipping in and out of consciousness, she looks toward Tony and Rick. Parts of their conversation reach her ears, but she finds it hard to distinguish what is real versus what is a hallucination.

Tony rubs his face, finally glad to get another update but disturbed by its contents. "All right, thanks for the heads up…. Understood." Tony snaps at his phone, ending the conversation with their NYPD mole.

"He quit the fucking force; believe that shit?"

Rick blinks a few times. "Who… what're you talking about?"

"Ravello, you idiot!" Tony skulks about the room, anger in every step. "Really fouled up the boss's plans."

"Why the hell'd he do that? Figured he be all happy after finally putting the boss away."

Tony halts. "Apparently Ravello's all fucked up health-wise."

Michelle's eyelids inch open, fluttering under the strain. Her breathing is shallow as drool collects on her bedsheets.

Rick, excited: "No shit? Maybe he kicks off," jerking his thumb toward Michelle's room, "and we can be done with her."

Tony grabs his partner by the shirt and growls, "We don't want that!"

Rick pulls his head back. "We don't?"

Tony stares Rick down before pushing him back and letting go. He pulls out a pack of cigarettes, tapping a Marlboro out and jabbing it at Rick. "Hell no. Ravello kicks, there goes the boss's plan to use them to escape." Tony slips the collection of carcinogens between his lips, lights up, and exhales a stream of smoke as he waves the cigarette. Smiling, he says sarcastically, "Only time you'll ever see the boss rooting for Ravello to pull through."

Rick smooths out his shirt, eyes Tony with caution. "He doing anything to get better?"

"Got some hotshot doc trying all sorts of experimental shit on him," Tony says impassively.

Rick nods. "Sounds like a crapshoot."

Tony laughs as Rick flinches. "It is. First treatment damn near killed him." Michelle's eyes go wide.

Rick, not knowing what to say, wishing this whole frigging mess was over, adds, "What's next?"

Tony stares back. "Good question." He takes a long drag on the cigarette and exhales. "He ain't shared any details with me yet." A wicked smile. "But this happened couple a weeks ago. If I know the boss, new plan he's working on has gotta be real good." Michelle's eyes go wide again at the next phrase. "Won't be long now before he's sprung and the Ravellos are pushing up daisies."

▷ Chapter 11 ◁

"Bottoms up, baby," Tony growls as Michelle takes the pill from him and with a sip of water and snap of her head sends it down her esophagus. "That a girl," he says as he reaches toward her gut, still laden with bruises from their earlier encounter, "lot easier on the belly then us forcing it."

Michelle nods and looks away, then finishes the water. "Can I go back to bed now?"

Tony glances at Rick, busy cleaning a frying pan filled minutes earlier with scrambled eggs, then back at the girl. "Suit yourself. One less thing for us to worry about."

Michelle drags her feet to the bedroom, Tony a step behind. He cuffs her to the bed, then closes the door on the way out as Michelle climbs into bed.

Strolling over to his orange juice, Tony downs it

and drops the glass in the sink next to his dish and silverware. Rick eyes the glass with annoyance, then grabs and cleans it. "Seems to be falling in line."

Tony plops down on the couch and grunts as he scratches himself. "'Bout time."

Rick busies himself with the rest of the dishes as Tony searches the TV in vain for an interesting movie or highlights from a ball game. Each man spends the next few minutes wrapped up in their own thoughts, not a word passing between them.

Michelle smiles at the sound of the TV going on, yet another example of the familiar routines the two thugs have fallen into. Without a sound she pulls a bobby pin out of her hair and unlocks the cuff, then slips out of bed and heads into the adjoining bathroom. She slides a finger down her throat, and moments later the sedative erupts from her stomach and lands in the sink, where Michelle rinses it off and dries it. She glides back to the bed and places the pill between the mattress and its fitted sheet, the first of many souvenirs she'll need.

▷ Chapter 12 ◁

Rick and Tony lay on opposite ends of the couch, nursing their respective hangovers. An empty bottle of Jack Daniel's sits on its side in the kitchen, a small pool of whiskey collected at the mouth of the bottle. Beer cans littler the dining room table and lay scattered on the floor.

Tony frees two aspirin from a bottle on the end table, then washes them down his throat as his hand clutches his head. "Aww, shit," he moans.

Rick slumps forward on his forearms, his face pasty and pale.

The morning news anchor's voice continues on in irritatingly upbeat fashion.

"With just four days till Christmas, shoppers are racing around, checking and rechecking their lists for last minute presents." A fake smile stretches from ear to ear. "Tourists line the streets of Rockefeller Plaza to glimpse this year's massive tree from Norway, while others window shop and take in the sights along Fifth Avenue."

Michelle is a crumpled mess. Immobile, her right hand is cuffed to the bed post, half her face buried in the sheets.

Rick's voice, pegged at just more than a whisper, rattles around Tony's head like a Kettle Drum. "Where we stand with things?"

Tony lifts his head from his hand. "Few more days and we oughtta be free of her." He staggers forward. "Ravello, he's done with a couple of treatments, feeling good 'bout himself." Tony clutches his head again and steadies himself on a chair as Michelle's eye opens, a smile breaking across the part of her face not shrouded by the sheets. "And the boss is doing his thing, dangling the missus so Ravello gets him the hell out of that hole." Michelle blinks twice, the smile receding as her eye narrows and her brow crinkles.

Rick nods his head in silence, happy to be free of her soon, determined to take what he wants before she goes.

▷ Chapter 13 ◁

Michelle spits out her latest force-fed pill and lifts up the mattress cover. She shakes her head as she eyes the five pills. Far less than she wanted. Turning the pills over one-by-one, she notes significant amounts of damage on three of them. Running through the calculations again, she tries to convince herself it will be enough. *No way to know for sure how much of an effect we'll get. Just have to plow ahead and hope for the best.*

She slips the spoon, pilfered during dinner, out of her underwear, gathers the pills, and begins crushing them on the end table under the dim illumination of the rickety old lamp. After several minutes she scrapes the powder from the table and guides it into the small Ziploc bag previously used to store tampons. Michelle slips the bag under the mattress cover, flicks off the light, and climbs into bed. She stares through the darkness toward the ceiling, her mind turning over every detail of her plan. The minutes tick by, her breath catching in her throat as she churns over the last of it. Everything needs to go right for this to work. Michelle bites her nails as she clutches her chest, trying to reassure herself.

And how often does that happen?

MICHELLE'S CAPTIVITY 4

FEROCITY

⊳ Chapter 1 ⊲

"**M**y honey always bought me flowers, 'specially on my birthday." Michelle slurs her words, her stupefied smile a testament to her steady diet of downers.

Rick, seated just a foot away on the couch, senses an opening and smiles agreeably. "That so? When's your birthday, sugar?"

Tony shakes his head with annoyance and raises the volume on the TV.

The smile again, the eyelashes batting erratically as her head lolls to one side. "December."

Rick laughs. "December what?"

"When are we now?" she struggles to keep her eyelids open.

Laughing again. "It's the 24th."

Tony squeezes the arms of his chair. He ups the volume a few more notches and glances at his watch. A few more minutes till his afternoon drink. He'll really need it today with these idiots.

Michelle looks at Rick sleepily, trying to make the connection. She giggles as she blurts it out. "Twenty-fourth? Like... uh, Christmas Eve, right?" The giggles come in full force now.

Rick whistles. "You got it."

Tony rolls his eyes.

More giggles, then Michelle struggling to be serious. "Birthday's to-mor-row."

Rick looks at her skeptically, then plays along. "What do you say I get you those flowers now?"

Tony starts to talk, then thinks better of it.

Her stoned face lights up. "Would you?"

"Maybe." Eyeing her lustily. "What's in it for me?"

She leans forward and tries to speak seductively as she winks and drags out the first word, "Whatever you want." She jabs her lips at his, the kiss smearing on his cheek by accident instead. Her head falls into his lap, tantalizing his groin.

Tony laughs. "Got a real live one there. Be careful she don't toss her cookies on ya before she passes out."

Rick grinds his hips toward her face, then sensing a need to move quickly before she passes out, he pulls her head back and plants a big kiss on her lips. Michelle's eyes go wide. Pulling away, a finger wagging at him in admonishment. "What about my flowers?" Shaking her head, she hiccups. "Deals a deal." The urge

170

to force himself on her right now is intense, but what a turn-on to have her willingly go down on him instead! He hesitates, then in a huff he says, "All right all ready." In one motion Rick gets up from the couch and grabs his coat off the table. "Be back in a few minutes, Tone."

"Whoa! You serious?" his partner says.

Pleading, he says, "Been like two months we had her and I ain't touched her..."

"Aw right, but make it quick." He reaches into his pocket and peels a twenty off of a roll of bills and tosses it to Rick. "Get me 'nother pack of Marlboro," then waves toward the implements. "And chain her up before ya go."

Rick says impatiently, "She's like a rag doll, sure we..." Tony's hard glare stops him. "Okay, okay." Rick grabs the shackles, fastens one pair to her wrists, the other to her ankles. Michelle purrs at him, "Mmmm, kinky." Rick stares at her, flustered and horny. "Be right back," and he bolts through the door.

Tony looks at his watch again. "Time for my drink." Michelle stumbles to her feet and skip-walks a wobbly path to the bottle. She grabs it, cap still on, and acts like she's guzzling it. "Woo-hoo, party!"

Tony jumps up and grabs the bottle from her, striking her across the face. "Gimme that." Michelle teeters, then falls into him, sending him stumbling back. Tony catches himself and pulls her off of him by the back of her head. He's ready to lash out, but she's already out cold.

"Christ." He drags her to the couch and throws her on it, drops the whiskey bottle on the end table, and trudges to the bathroom to clean up.

§

Rick hurries along the street in search of the goods. He spots a bodega and smiles, but the smile fades as he approaches and sees the CLOSED sign. "What the hell?" A Hispanic man passing by blurts out, "Christmas Eve, man, ain't nobody hardly open." Rick shakes his head and waves an acknowledgment to the man.

His eyes search the block ahead. Deserted and not one business open. He hustles onward. Maybe it'll be different a few blocks over.

§

The door to the john slamming shut, Michelle makes her move. Pulling the Ziploc out of her pants she twists the cap off the bottle and dumps the powder into it, then stuffs the baggie under the seat cushion. The toilet flushes. Michelle recaps the bottle and shakes it vigorously then falls back onto the couch as Tony finishes washing up and comes out of the bathroom. He eyes her, then his bottle, and moves toward the kitchen for a glass, not noticing the last few air bubbles popping atop the whiskey. Plodding back to the couch,

Tony drops himself on it and exhales, grumbling, "'Bout fucking time I get some peace." Michelle cracks open one lid, a faint, involuntary smile forming as he downs a tall glass of the drink and readies another.

§

Six blocks away, near the corner of 72nd Avenue and 110th Street, Rick finds a 7-Eleven open. With long strides he approaches the counter, calling out to the man in a turban, "Pack of Marlboros. Got any flowers?"

The man does a funny head shake/nod thing. "Only Marlboro lights. Okay?"

Rick shakes his head and curses to himself. "What else ya got?"

"Camel, Lucky Strikes, Newport..."

"Gimme the Camel." Then he says impatiently, "Flowers?"

The man points toward the back of the store, then turns and grabs the cigarettes.

Rick rolls his eyes and stomps away from the counter, his footsteps echoing along the narrow, empty aisle.

§

Tony's glass slips from his hand and crashes to the floor as his head falls back. A split second later Michelle pounces, her hands diving into his pockets in search of the key for the chains. She spills his pockets onto the couch and floor. Coins and an old comb scatter at Tony's feet. The keys slide toward the crack in the couch between seat and back cushion. Michelle lunges toward the keys as they disappear in the crack. "Shit." Her hands dive in after them, searching frantically.

Tony stirs.

So soon? How's it possible?

Michelle's fingertips latch onto the keys. She rips them from the couch crack and fumbles with the lock on her wrists as Tony groans, his hand rising to his head. She pushes the key in, jiggles it in the lock.

For God's sake, c'mon!

Tony's eyes blink open as Michelle frees one hand, then the other. The shackles fall to the couch and then clang on the floor. Tony grabs Michelle's wrist. "What the hell?" he says, knocking the keys clear across the floor.

$

Rick glances over the flower selection, an array of weeds that looks days old. He yanks a bunch from the stand and marches back to the counter. A moment later he pays and heads out the door, anxious to get back and claim his prize before her mood changes or she passes out.

§

Tony throws his weight on Michelle, driving the breath from her as she slams into the couch's armrest. His hands encircle her throat, squeezing the flesh between them like a boa constrictor. "You fuckin' bitch!" Michelle's hands are a blur as her nails stab at his face and eyes. Blood spurts from his cheeks as Tony screams and releases his grip. Michelle plunges her nails into his jowls and with a twisting motion and a knee to his groin, sends him crashing to the floor.

Tony's head strikes the floor with a hideous thud. His arms and legs go limp as Michelle scurries away. Her head darts back and forth, her eyes scouring the floor for the keys, for anything else that can be useful.

She finds nothing.

Panicked, she forgets about the chains on her feet and comes crashing to the floor as she turns to run away.

§

Rick's steps are filled with purpose and power. His feet slam into the sidewalk's pavement. Peering ahead he sees it's just a few more blocks to go. Two or three seconds and the building will come into focus in the distance.

§

Michelle jabs at the buzzer on the old elevator again and again. With no way of knowing where it is in its journey, she heads off for the stairs, the chains and shackles clanking as she takes awkward stutter steps. Seconds shoot by, her adrenaline pumping as she pushes herself to move faster, knowing Rick could be back any moment.

She hobbles down the first flight of stairs, scurrying along the landing. As she reaches her leg down toward the next step, the chains get tangled. Michelle comes crashing down. A flurry of arms, legs, torso, and head careen down the stairs before she slams onto the cold, hard entryway on the building's first floor. No time to lose, Michelle struggles to her feet and moves briskly toward the door. Hand on the door handle, her eye catches movement through the large pane glass on one side of the door. *Shit!* Rick's just down the street and coming toward her fast!

Her eyes sweep the building's interior. She ducks into the small mailroom as Rick bounds up the stairs and pushes through the front door.

§

The front door crashes into the wall next to Michelle. She pulls in her breath and body, flattening it against the wall as Rick powers forward and climbs up the stairs. Michelle shudders as the sound of his footsteps fade. No time to lose. She scurries out of the room and through the front door, hoping her small lead on him will hold.

§

Rick barges through the door, flowers extended in front of him. "Look what I got for some—" His eyes jump to the floor, to Tony's body sprawled out and still. "What the fuck?" He tosses the flowers aside and falls to the floor, shaking his partner's bloody face. "Tone, Tone. Wake up." Rick slaps his face hard, worried his friend may be dead. Tony's eyes shoot open as his hand grabs Rick's. "What the hell?"

Rick: "How long you been out? What happened?"

"How the fuck should I know?" Rick helps Tony sit up, as the bloodied man's eyes scan the room. "She's gone."

"What're we gonna do?"

Tony struggles to his feet. His eyes catch one set of chains on the floor as he remembers the altercation. "Let's go. Her feet are still chained. Couldn't have gotten far."

The men start toward the door, Tony freezing as he feels a jiggling in his pocket. Rick pulls up and looks back at his partner as Tony glances at the phone. This is the last thing they need right now.

§

"Here's the burner you asked for," Kennedy grumbles as he tosses it into the back seat. "Now set up that damn meet." Durand, handcuffed to the inside of the door of Kennedy's Civic, punches the phone number in as he leans against the door.

§

Tony jabs at the phone and tentatively holds it to his ear. The voice is unmistakable. "Ready her. Detective Kennedy and I will meet you in a half hour."

"We got a big problem, Boss. The girl's escaped. We're going out to find her." Tony cringes in anticipation of the verbal assault.

"Yes, the field by the abandoned warehouse, near the dock that goes to North Brother Island."

Tony's brain is frozen. Didn't Durand hear him? What the hell's he supposed to do? He takes a couple of breaths, his mind whirling through his options. Looking at his partner, he says, "Gotta meet the boss. Go get her, and I'll catch up later." Rick nods and disappears through the door in a flash, hoping she hasn't gotten far.

§

Michelle hobbles west along 110th street, wondering where the hell she is. She looks up at the cross street, confused: 69th Road, and a block ahead, 69th Avenue. Only Queens has such an odd pattern of roads, streets, and avenues. The chains biting into her ankles, her feet covered only by a pair of thin athletic socks, she squints. *Up ahead, a small pay phone station? What luck!*

She hurries forward, knowing even without money she can call 911. As Michelle reaches the station, her face falls. A torn cord hangs from the phone, the receiver nowhere in sight. "Oh no," she cries as tears spring up. What now? She looks all around as she wipes her eyes and curses her luck. Not a person to be found. Not one business open. How cruel; Christmas Eve and help nowhere in sight!

§

Rick takes the stairs in a blur and crashes through the building's front door. His eyes and head swivel every which way as he grumbles to himself. "Christ, he's gonna kill us if I don't find her." Rick starts off to the left, cupping his hands like binoculars over his eyes. No sign of her! He stops, turns to the right. Maybe that direction? Shit! Shit! How can he know?

A scream to his left. Rick turns and peers in the distance.

§

Michelle spots a beat up, badly damaged brick building just ahead. Maybe a place to hide. Her foot crunches forward, recoiling in pain as she screams, her eyes darting to small shards of glass on the ground. She shakes and wipes pieces from her sock. *What's that?*

She reaches for the thin, twisted piece of metal. A small paper clip. *Might work.*

She grabs it and thrusts it into the shackle around one leg, popping the lock on the first try. She hears footsteps far off in the distance but coming her way. Her eyes dart toward them. *Rick? Oh no! Got to hurry.*

She fidgets with the other lock, her cold hands getting numb. The footsteps grow faster, louder. One final try. The chains fall from her foot! Without even glancing back, she races toward the alley next to the building.

§

Rick sees something, somebody off in the distance. Crouched down near the ground. *Is it her? Is it even a woman? Hard to tell from so far away.* He makes one last survey of the entire area. No one else in sight in any direction. Nothing to lose, he walks briskly toward the figure. Getting closer the details begin to emerge. Definitely not a kid. Man or woman? Ten strides more. Woman. Definitely. Fumbling with something. *It's her!*

Getting the shackles off. Rick takes off in a full out run as he sees Michelle do the same.

Just one block away, Rick sees Michelle disappear down an alleyway. He turns on the speed, his legs and arms a blur, the burn of lactic acid filling his limbs as he closes the gap. He slows as he makes the turn into the alleyway. Up ahead he sees her jumping onto the end of the second-floor fire escape ladder. Now's his chance!

Powering forward, he's just a few feet away as she pulls herself up the ladder, feet still dangling in the air.

He lunges toward those feet.

But Michelle is ready.

Holding the ladder tight she swings her legs back and propels them forward, delivering a crushing blow to Rick's jaw that sends him flying backward. He crashes into the ground and slams his head into a large garbage bin as Michelle gets her footing and flies up the ladder. She races across the landing, up the steps, landing, steps again. Scurrying by dirty, decrepit windows on the top floor, she looks up.

Damn! No way to reach the roof.

Michelle looks down. Rick's already up, pitifully trying to jump up and catch the ladder. A brief flash of her smile. White men can't jump syndrome. She looks all around. No way up. No sense going back down. What to do? Rick gets behind the garbage bin, straining to move it. Nothing at first, then a slight motion. He lets out a roar, pushes it close to the ladder, and flips the top shut.

Michelle stares down in horror as Rick lunges, catches the ladder, and holds on for dear life. She's got to move now! Grabbing at the window, she strains to open it as Rick teeters, then steadies himself and makes the climb up.

On the first landing he stops to catch his breath as a call comes through and says, "The abandoned building two blocks west. On the fire escape."

Michelle looks at the window then down at him. She backs up, closes her eyes, and plows forward, glass flying everywhere as she tumbles through. "Strike that. In the building, top floor. See you inside in a minute."

Rick charges up the fire escape as Michelle scampers to her feet, cursing the glass cutting into her as she takes off. Rats scurry ahead of her as she shrieks and barrels out of the apartment, into the hallway. Seconds later Rick enters the window, careful to avoid cutting himself on the glass. A sick smile forms on his face.

Won't be long now.

§

Tony throws the car into park as he skids onto the curb, sending trash cans flying. He reaches into the glove box, pulls out a small pistol, and jumps out of the car. Best thing would be to take her alive. But if that's not possible...

§

Michelle's heart pounds with fear as she tears down the stairwell. Rick's boots hammer ever closer, each reverberation amplifying her anxiety as she dodges gaps in the rotted wood. Lunging onto the next landing, she stumbles and slams into the floor. Panic overtakes her as she scrambles to her feet with Rick bearing down on her. *One more set of stairs, then I can outrun him on the street!* But Michelle's heart sinks as the front door flies open. Tony comes crashing in, gun drawn. His beady eyes lock in on Michelle, unaware Rick is close behind her.

Only one chance to get out of this alive. Michelle pauses a split second, waiting till Rick is almost on top of her but still out of Tony's line of sight. *It's now or never. Here goes...*

She reaches into her pants for a nonexistent weapon, and turns her head backward as she yells, "You won't take me alive," just as Rick lunges toward her, intent on smothering and subduing her.

Tony raises his gun, gets her in his sights and rips off two shoots. But Michelle anticipates the shots, flattens herself against the landing just in time as Rick's body flies forward, grabbing at empty air.

One bullet rips through his chest, the other his head, killing him instantly. Rick's body crashes to the ground, sliding along the landing before tumbling over and over down the stairs. Tony, stunned, runs forward to meet his partner. "Aw shit!" Michelle stays pressed against the floor.

Tony stares at Rick's lifeless face, then let's out a furious scream as he climbs the stairs and trains his gun on Michelle. "Don't fucking move, bitch, 'less you wanna end up like him!" Tony yanks her up by her hair and pulls her head back. Michelle raises her hands and cries, "Don't shoot!" just as his right hand and gun collide violently with her face. Blood spurts out of her mouth as she feels his hot breath on her neck. "Oughtta drop you right now, but the boss has got other plans." He shoves her ahead, down the stairs and through the door. At the car he throws her in the front passenger's seat and pushes her across to the wheel. Slamming the door shut, he tosses her the keys. "Drive."

§

The minutes race by as Michelle drives toward the launching point for North Brother Island, Tony's firearm trained on her. "Why'd you let me live back there when Rick died?" she asks.

"Don't worry, toots, you ain't long for this world," he says with a gruff laugh.

Michelle stares at him, her face a mix of fear and confusion.

"You're the boss's bait. He's using you to get your husband to spring him." The laugh again. "For a doc your hubby ain't too bright sometimes."

Michelle glares at him.

"Boss got your man thinking he can help solve some frigging murder case your chump's working on."

"He can't?"

"Fuck no!" Tony scratches his cheek with the back of his hand. "That and your little happy reunion were just excuses to get him sprung."

Michelle nods her head as she peers ahead at the sparse traffic.

"Soon as we reunite you lovebirds—POW!—we off you both and make our escape."

Michelle shudders, her mind racing, searching for a way out.

She comes up empty.

§

"Pull off up here," Tony barks with a wave of his gun as they approach the gated North Brother Island launch point. "Now gimme the keys," he says as Michelle shifts the Town Car into park. The thug exits the car, wind whipping at his face as he circles over to the driver's side window and raps on it. "Come on. We ain't got all night." Michelle's worried eyes find his, then avert as she climbs out of the vehicle, Tony backing up so she can't make a play for his gun. He juts his chin forward. "After you, toots."

Michelle enters the code in the keypad, the

gate mechanism engaging with a loud screech, then creaking open as the two of them squeeze through. The thug looks at Chris's car with disdain as he slides past it. "Thought they was being real cute, blocking the entrance so we can't come storming in after them."

Michelle moves forward without a word, Tony's gun pointed at the center of her back, his breathing heavy as her mind continues its vain search for a way to break free. They quickly traverse the lot and climb into the boat, Tony's gun trained on her chest as she powers up the outboard motor and steers through the crisp night air toward North Brother Island.

Moonlight streams down on them as they tie up and hustle across the small beach. Tony spews expletives as they work their way through the thicket, then onto the dilapidated structure that houses Hyslop's lab. The gangster pauses at the front door to catch his breath and wipe his brow as he sizes Michelle up and pushes her forward with a wave of the gun.

Flipping the entryway light on, their footsteps echo along the deserted corridor as they find their way to the lab. Unbeknownst to them, a gun is brandished inside the lab as a tense standoff ensues. But out in the hallway an eerie, unsettling silence is all that fills the air. Concern etched on his face, Tony pushes forward and with a gruff voice snaps, "Outta the way, toots." Michelle complies, Tony peering through the glass opening in the door. His frown transforms into a wide grin as he grabs the door handle and leans back. Michelle takes a deep breath. Her heart skips a beat, then two, as he slowly turns the knob. Trepidation fills her heart as Tony pulls the door open while waving her forward. She takes a step, then halts as her eyes meet his, his grin turning into a sick, self-satisfied sneer. Her lips start to move, but Tony shoves her forward, the protest dying in her throat as she stumbles forward into the fray....

§

After months of anguish, heartache, and hopelessness, a tidal wave of euphoria and relief crashes through Chris. "Michelle!" He cries out with an all-encompassing smile as tears run down his face. "Thank God you're alive!" Overwhelmed by utter, blissful disbelief, he's transfixed by her beauty.

Tears well in Michelle's eyes. Her heart bursts with joy and relief, but something is amiss. "Chris! Watch it. It's a trap," she yells. Aching to hold her, Chris starts toward her anyway, then sees Durand's goon, his gun jammed into her back.

"Stop right there, Ravello, or she gets it." He pushes Michelle forward. "Time to disarm, detectives. Ravello, you first. Slide your gun away on the counter." As Chris complies, the goon adds, "Thatta boy. Now Kennedy, turn your gun backwards and hand it to my Boss along with the keys to them cuffs."

Kennedy angrily passes his Glock and the keys to Durand. The sociopath undoes the cuffs, making a show of dropping them to the floor, then slides behind Kennedy and jabs the gun into his back.

Durand: "Now, that's more like it." He nudges Kennedy toward Zigler. "I'm going to need that test tube now, Mr. Zigler."

Todd's eyes dart between Durand and his henchman as Todd clutches the glass tube and backs away.

Durand pushes Kennedy off to the side, opening up a clear path to Zigler. He creeps forward. "Nothing to worry about, Todd. I'm not going to hurt you. All I want is the detective's cure, and then you'll be free to go." Durand smiles and extends his hand. "Just give it to me and off you go. Honor among criminals, and all that good stuff, right Toddy?"

"The second you give it to him, you're a dead man," Chris yells.

Todd mumbles, "I never even met him before." He stops backpedaling, then reaches out to Durand with the compound. "How could he want me dead?"

Durand steps forward. "How indeed?" He shakes his head. "Ravello just doesn't want me to have his precious medication." He motions to Todd to hand it over. Todd steps forward, placing the tube in his hand. Durand looks Todd in the eyes. "There, that wasn't so hard, was it?" The sociopath secures the medication and starts to turn away, then twists back and fires on

188

Todd, the bullet tearing through his right eye. Todd falls to the ground, dead.

Durand slips Chris's cure into his coat pocket. "Shame on you, dear doctor-detective." He shakes his head. "Trying to warn Zigler like that."

"Why would you kill him, Durand? He didn't even know you, for God's sake."

Durand shakes his head. "It's what I do, Detective. I'm one of the bad guys, remember?" His face turns icy cold. "And bad guys kill people."

Chris glances at Kennedy and see his hand edging toward his jacket pocket. Could he have another gun?

Durand's eyes trace Ravello's line of sight, setting off a whirlwind of motion. "He's got a gun, stop him!"

Michelle jabs her elbow into her captor's solar plexus, hitting him over the head as he doubles over in pain, the gun flying out of his hand. Kennedy fumbles in his jacket for the gun as the gangster straightens up and lunges at him, slamming into Kennedy just as he frees the pistol from his pocket. The two men roll around on the ground, struggling for control of the firearm.

Chris takes a quick step toward Durand, then ducks for cover as he fires wildly on him. Three shots ring out. Glass shatters and flies all around him. Chris stays low as caustic chemicals and powders cover the coun-tertops, dripping onto the floor. A burner topples over, igniting the chemicals. Flames race across the wood countertop in every direction. Kennedy rolls on top as his adversary, in control of the gun, takes aim. Kev strikes his hands just as he's firing, sending another bullet past Chris. A loud thud reverberates to Chris's left as Durand takes aim at Kennedy. Michelle yells "Duck!" just as Durand pulls his own trigger. Kennedy gets clear just in time, as Durand's bullet strikes his man dead. Flames rise up from the ground, overtaking the countertops, running up the walls as Durand eludes Kennedy's flailing hands and jumps over the dead man's body. The door to the lab opens, the rush of oxygen into the room fanning the flames as Durand escapes. Off to Chris's left he sees Hyslop on the ground, injured but moving.

Chris yells out, "Kev, grab Michelle and get the hell out of here! I gotta get Hyslop." He hears Michelle's cries. "No, Chris! Leave him!" Chris half hears, half sees Kennedy fight his way over to Michelle and subdue her as she struggles to break free to save him.

"Get out now, Michelle, before it's too late! I'll find my own way." Flames lick the air in front of her, illuminating her face and the beautiful scar on her neck that brought her back to Chris. As Kennedy drags her away, Chris hears his partner's voice. "No way out. Too many fucking flames... Hold on, what if I..." Kennedy's primordial scream rings out as he grabs the thug's dead body, jerking it off the ground with one hand as he holds Michelle with the other. Using the body as a shield, Kennedy guides Michelle and himself out of the lab. Chris hears their footsteps receding as he crawls over to Hyslop, hoping, praying there's still time to save them both.

⯈ **Chapter 2** ⯇

Kennedy explodes through the front door of the burning building, flames shooting after him, the smell of burned flesh in his grasp. Gasping for air, the body slips from his grip as he and Michelle stagger to safety, then collapse to the ground. A full minute passes before either stirs.

Kennedy looks up first, pushing Tony's charred body away. Michelle lies face down, motionless. Kennedy swallows hard and tentatively reaches out for her. His hand touches her arm.

"Michelle, are you okay?"

Silence.

Tears gather in Kennedy's eyes as he turns her over and leans into her chest to listen for breathing.

Nothing.

Suddenly coughing, sweet merciful coughing, as Michelle lurches forward!

"Oh God... passed out." Michelle's eyes search the area. She sees the dead body, smoke rising off its charred flesh. "Chris! No!"

Kennedy intercepts her, shakes his head. "Not him." He points. "He's still in there. I'm gonna get 'im."

Michelle nods, emotion choking the words in her throat as tears stream down her face.

Kennedy stumbles to his feet, staggering forward as the front of the building, engulfed in flames, collapses before their horrified eyes. Wood and brick crash to the ground in a series of loud thuds. Sparks and embers fly everywhere, leaving no way into—or out of—the building.

❯ Chapter 3 ❮

hris slings Hyslop's still body across his shoulders and plows through the flames, hoping against hope to find a path out. Smoke stings Chris's eyes as the pungent order and taste of ashes assault his senses. Coughing, eyes tearing, lungs on fire, Ravello staggers forward, through the lab door. Flames jump out and recede in front of him. No use trying to dodge their unpredictable paths. Searing pain fills the detective's body as the fire scalds him with each step. Hyslop's weight bears down on him, threatening to stop Chris dead in his tracks.

Up ahead Chris glimpses it—the rotunda. Only ten, fifteen feet to go after that. The detective yells as he trudges forward into the circular space. Flames rush up the walls, engulfing the ceiling. Smoke obliterates his view. Chris takes two steps, then it happens. A blinding light ahead, fire everywhere, eating the building alive. Beams crash down in front of him.

▷ Chapter 4 ◁

Kennedy stops dead in his tracks as the front of the building collapses to the ground. Michelle runs toward it. "No! Chris!" The detective intercepts her, Michelle's fists pounding his chest to let her go. She shrieks, her words unintelligible as Kennedy drags her back to safety.

"Stay here." Kennedy rushes toward the left side of the building, toward the lab itself. He frantically searches for a way in, but the jutting flames hold him back. Smoke billows before him as the ground trembles. Suddenly, an ear-shattering, concussive blow sends Kennedy flying backward as the lab explodes, hurling debris and equipment through the air. Glass, wood, brick, and metal rain down around Kennedy as Michelle shrieks louder.

Moments later a smaller explosion, then another,

rock the lab. Kennedy struggles to his feet, hoping against hope for a way to save Chris. He pulls back from the building and scans the area for a way in. There isn't any.

Michelle, a few feet away, falls to her knees, her hands clawing at the dirt, tears pouring over her ash-covered face. No way Chris survived this. Her screams die in her throat, her voice overwhelmed by a piercing anguish. She crumbles to the ground face first, sobbing, spent, and defeated, her will to live all but gone.

Thirty seconds goes by, then thirty more. Kennedy leans over, speaking softly to Michelle. Slowly, she lifts her head and stares into the abyss of the raging fire, her spirit destroyed.

Kennedy tries to console Michelle as he helps her to her feet, but it's futile.

On the right side of the building glass shatters. Motion. An animal? Michelle blinks, refocuses, straining to see. "Oh my God! Chris?" She sprints toward his beleaguered body as he crawls away from the wreckage. Kennedy races over, spotting Hyslop's still body several feet behind Chris. He grabs the scientist and hauls him away from the fire as Michelle wraps her arms around Chris. "Thank God! Thank God you're all right. I thought you were dead." Michelle smothers him with tear-drenched kisses as Chris smiles feebly and mouths "My baby" as he collapses in her arms.

§

"This is Detective Kevin Kennedy of the 1-7. We have an officer and scientist down on North Brother Island. Repeat, officer and scientist down on North Brother Island. Send EMS and the FDNY. Building is burning to the ground, injuries may be life-threatening." Kennedy catches his breath as he looks at the dock, the remaining boat doused in flames. "Also need an APB on Jean Louis Durand, aka "The Giver," presumed to have fled the island via boat about twenty minutes ago."

Kennedy hobbles over to Ravello, a concerned look on his face as he sees Chris buried in Michelle's arms. "How is he?"

Michelle smiles back, her arms holding Chris tight. "Exhausted but alive."

"Just called for EMS, FDNY. Not sure how long it'll take them to get—What the fuck?" Kennedy's head snaps to attention as several boats approach the shore. They bypass the dock with its burning boat. As they run aground, Commissioner John Kelly disembarks, walking purposefully toward Kennedy. Medics stream out of the other boats, racing toward Ravello and Hyslop. "Cavalry is here, Detective. How are you holding up?"

"Hanging in there, sir. How'd you get here so quickly? I just called it in," Kennedy says.

Kelly points toward Ravello, EMT's caring for him

and Hyslop as they ready them for transport. "Chris sent word earlier about his plan, asked us to stake out Port Morris for when Durand tried to escape."

Kennedy smiles. "You got him?"

Kelly's face fills with satisfaction. "We did." The commissioner uses his right hand to crack the knuckles in his left. "Fucker thought he'd outwitted us when he got off the boat and tried to grab his car and go." A broad smile on his face now. "Till we converged on him like feeding time at the zoo." Kelly laughs. "Two officers are running him back to Rikers as we speak." Kelly juts his chin toward the burning building. "What happened here?"

"Durand killed our perp on the Malekoviec and Richards murders, then lit up the place on the way out." Kennedy's face registers fear as the realization hits him. "Shit, the lab workers and secretary never got out."

Kelly places a hand on Kennedy's shoulder. "Relax, Detective. We found them a few minutes ago. Chris sent them out before the fireworks started, telling them to hover off shore in the boats until we arrived." Medics hustle by, loading Chris and the doctor for transport. Moments later everyone sets off for the mainland, the fire raging on like an ominous beacon in the eerie, dark night.

§

Kev, Michelle, and Chris commiserate on shore as EMT's speed off into the night with Hyslop, siren and lights blaring. A few officers mill about, overseeing the impounding of Durand's car. Kelly waves to the detectives and Michelle as he slips into his Town Car and leaves the scene.

Kev turns to his partner. "Clear something up for me."

"What's that?"

"Zigler's plan, setting up St. James to make it look like she was setting up Gorelick while also making Hyslop look suspicious." He shakes his head. "Pretty involved. How'd you know for sure you were reading things right?"

"McCarthy."

"McCarthy?" Kennedy says with surprise.

"Sent me a text while we were taking the boat out to the island."

"What'd it say?"

"Found it just like you said."

Kennedy shakes his head. Michelle and he look at Chris.

"I was pretty sure Zigler was our man but not a hundred percent. So I had McCarthy go to Zigler's apartment to find the proof."

"And?" they say in unison.

"No way Zigler could taint the medicines, kill his vics without a lot of trial and error. And he sure as hell couldn't test out his theories at Hyslop's lab."

Kennedy: "So you told McCarthy he'd find a small lab there, and that would cinch it?"

"Bingo. And that's just what he found, right down to the notebooks Zigler kept on his experiments with some unlucky rodents," Chris says with a laugh.

"Nice," Kennedy says with appreciation.

The next minute drifts by in silence before Michelle, looking out toward the island, cuts in, "Can't believe how fast it burned to the ground." She shakes her head and says in a somber tone, "All the good work being done there, destroyed in a few minutes." Brightening, she hugs Chris. "Thank God we made it out alive."

Kennedy chimes in, "Your cure, too." He smiles. "Durand left with a vial of it. 'Bout time that fucker did something right."

Michelle, excited: "That's right! You're overdue for your last dose. Should we get the medicine tonight?"

Chris waves her off. "Nah. They'll confiscate it at Rikers. We can get it in the morning. No way Jacobs would be giving it to me before then anyway."

Michelle: "Tomorrow's Christmas, Chris."

"Aw shit, I forgot!" Chris shakes his head in frustration, then does his best to try and laugh it off. "Fortunately, Jacobs is Jewish. Maybe he'll do me a favor and shoot me up after Mass."

Michelle offers a disapproving smile and shakes her head. "We can only hope."

A minute passes in silence, then Kennedy asks,

"Why do you think Durand offed Zigler? The guy didn't even know him."

"Not sure, but my gut tells me we're dealing with something much bigger than meets the eye," Chris says, "and knowing Durand, he's at the center of it."

A medic approaches, handing them each towels to clean up. "Need anything else?"

Chris glances at Kennedy then side hugs Michelle. "No, I've got all I'll ever need." Reaching out a hand, he adds, "Thank you for all your help."

The medic nods and trudges off. Finally a moment to themselves! Chris takes Michelle's hand in his, slowly caressing then kissing it before he envelopes her in a soulful hug neither of them wants to end. When at last it does, Chris loses himself in her beautiful blue eyes, feeling eternally grateful that she somehow cheated death, not once but twice. He takes a slow, deep breath, cupping her chin in his hands, then their lips intertwine as they enjoy a passionate kiss that takes her breath away. At the sound of Kev's coughing they come up for air, both embarrassed by their public display of affection. Hoping to ease his buddy's selfconsciousness, Chris plays it casual. "Hell of a night, huh?"

"Hell of a few months," Michelle chimes in as she rolls her eyes. Then smiling, she says, "Let's get home, baby."

Chris nods. "Best idea I've heard in weeks." He turns to Kennedy and shakes his hand as he pats Kennedy's shoulder. "Great job, partner."

Kennedy breaks out in a knowing smile as he eyes both of them. "Merry Christmas, guys. Now get outta here before you two get arrested for public indecency."

▷ Chapter 5 ◁

Chris places a quick call to his Dad as he and Michelle climb into the Firebird and drive through the gate. "...We'll be there soon. But Dad, it's very important you talk to the kids about their big surprise. Christine and James are so young. I don't want them to be frightened or confused so here's what you should tell them...."

The next forty-five minutes speeds by as they wind their way north of The City to Peekskill. Michelle and Chris hold hands, her dozing off intermittently as they enjoy the first moments of peace since raiding Durand's lab months ago. Chris smiles at his wife as they exit Route 9 at South Street, then a few minutes later pull into their driveway.

Climbing the stairs to the porch, Chris feels a vibration in his pocket. He frees his phone and looks at the number with annoyance. *Just going to have to wait.* At the front door Chris pauses and kisses Michelle softly. Then he steps in, hiding Michelle behind him as he places his keys and phone on a small table next to the door. His dad is sitting in a chair in the living room, the kids on each side of him, reading "The Little Engine That Could."

Chris smiles from ear to ear. "God's given us the most wonderful, beautiful Christmas present ever." He steps aside and their faces light up as Michelle comes forward and drops down to her knees. "Mommy!" they scream as they rush toward her. Tears of joy stream down everyone's faces as the kids hug Michelle for dear life. She kisses them all over. "My babies, mommy loves you so, so much." Chris wraps his arms around Michelle, Christine, and James, then leans back and waves his dad over. "What's a family hug without Grandpa?" he says with a broad smile.

Arms interlocked in the tightest of group hugs, Chris can hardly breathe but he has never felt better, freer, or happier.

In the midst of their revelry, Chris hears the phone dancing on the stand next to them, its incessant vibrations impossible to ignore. The detective curses under his breath as he breaks from the family hug. *What disaster is so bad that it can't wait til the friggin' morning?* His jaw falls open as he reads Kev's text.

THE END

§

Never Miss A Sale, Preorder, Or New Release!
Follow Me On Bookbub:

https://www.bookbub.com/authors/william-rubin

ABOUT THE AUTHOR

William Rubin is a practicing physician who enjoys weaving tales of medical/scientific intrigue. Writing for him is equal parts catharsis, creativity, and escape from the rigors of a busy medical practice and the joys and challenges of raising a family.

The works of James Patterson, Robin Cook, Michael Palmer, and Patricia Cornwell inspired Dr. Rubin to create the Chris Ravello Medical Thriller Series. Each book in the series has regularly enjoyed a place on the Amazon Best Sellers lists for Medical Thrillers and Medical Fiction since their releases.

Challenges and tragedies in Dr. Rubin's life, particularly the untimely death of his mother, provided some of the underlying drama, conflict, and turmoil for the series' lead character.

When he isn't busy practicing medicine or crafting his next medical thriller, Dr. Rubin enjoys time with his family and friends, running, playing piano, and traveling.

To find out more about William and what is coming next for Chris Ravello, visit the author on Facebook (william.erubin), Twitter (https://twitter.com/werubin671), or follow him on Goodreads, Amazon, or Bookbub. You can also email him (werubin67@gmail.com) to receive a link to sign-up for his newsletter.

William values your thoughts, insights, and feelings on *Michelle's Captivity*, so please post a review on your favorite websites/blogs.

ACKNOWLEDGMENT

Once again, many thanks to my work team for their invaluable help. They are:

Dee Gott: Beta Reading

Christine Keleny: formatting and editorial work

Anne Pottinger: proofreading

Carl Graves at Extended Imagery: cover design

And on the home-front, to Eilene, Diane, and James for all your patience, understanding, and inspiration.

DISCUSSION GUIDE

1) What are the main themes in *Michelle's Captivity*?

2) What things stood out most for you in this story? Why?

3) What are your thoughts about Michelle's captors, Rick and Tony?

4) If you were Michelle Ravello, would you have done anything differently?

5) What parts of Michelle's journey resonated the most with you and why?

6) How did you feel about Michelle Ravello's return and how it was handled?

7) Would you like to read other stories where Michelle

is the lead character? If so, are there particular area(s) of Michelle's life, past or present, you would like to learn more about?

8) How do you think the tremendous trauma Michelle went through has changed her? How do you think these traumas will shape Michelle's life going forward?

9) Did you enjoy the balance between medical thriller and family saga in the story?